CAST OF CHARACTERS

*Five extraordinary siblings. One dangerous past.
Unlimited potential.*

Susannah Hobson—Her stepmother's suspicious death has turned her world upside down, and she discovers everyone has secrets—even the ruggedly handsome rancher who has vowed to protect her and her unborn chid, whether she likes it or not!

Travis Dean—He'd left the city and come to his grandfather's ranch to get away from trouble, only to encounter his proud, willful and very pregnant neighbor, who badly needed someone to watch over her—and give her a lasting lesson in love.

Williard Croft—The ruthless mastermind behind Violet's untimely death will stop at nothing to hunt down the Extraordinary Five—even if it means destroying everyone they love.

Jake Ingram—He couldn't believe Violet was gone, not when he'd just reunited with his loving birth mother. His hopes of unlocking the mysteries of his extraordinary past vanished with her death, unless...

About the Author

CINDY GERARD

Two RITA® Award finalist books and a National Reader's Choice Award are among the many highlights of Cindy Gerard's career. This bestselling author of over twenty category titles is delighted to release her first Silhouette single title continuity, *The Bluewater Affair,* book four of the FAMILY SECRETS series.

Cindy will be the first to tell you that writing full-time has its perks—for instance, going to work in your jammies if the mood strikes you—but it also has its downsides. The solitude can sometimes feel overwhelming. That's one of the reasons Cindy was so excited by the invitation to contribute to the FAMILY SECRETS project. The unique and compelling story line linking the books together came with an unspoken "reach out and touch someone" clause. Participating authors were in constant contact with each other during the creation of these intriguing stories; the new relationships built around those contacts are golden nuggets Cindy treasures.

Cindy invites you to sit back and settle in for a wild, romantic ride. If you enjoy reading the FAMILY SECRETS books half as much as Cindy enjoyed writing her contribution to the series, you're in for an amazing journey. Visit Cindy at: www.cindygerard.com.

CINDY GERARD

THE BLUEWATER
AFFAIR

Silhouette Books

Published by Silhouette Books
America's Publisher of Contemporary Romance

Special thanks and acknowledgment are given
to Cindy Gerard for her contribution
to the FAMILY SECRETS series.

 SILHOUETTE BOOKS

ISBN 0-373-61371-7

THE BLUEWATER AFFAIR

FAMILY SECRETS

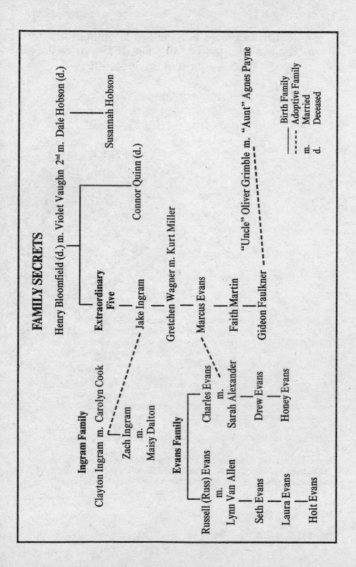

Henry Bloomfield (d.) m. Violet Vaughn 2ⁿᵈ m. Dale Hobson (d.)

Susannah Hobson

Extraordinary Five

Connor Quinn (d.)

Jake Ingram

Gretchen Wagner m. Kurt Miller

Marcus Evans

Faith Martin

Gideon Faulkner

"Uncle" Oliver Grimble m. "Aunt" Agnes Payne

Ingram Family

Clayton Ingram m. Carolyn Cook

Zach Ingram
m.
Maisy Dalton

Evans Family

Charles Evans
m.
Sarah Alexander

Drew Evans

Honey Evans

Russell (Russ) Evans
m.
Lynn Van Allen

Seth Evans

Laura Evans

Holt Evans

———— Birth Family
-------- Adoptive Family
m. Married
d. Deceased

This book is dedicated to my intrepid,
incredibly talented FAMILY SECRETS cybersisters.
Ladies—you're the greatest!

Prologue

Late March, Sheridan, Wyoming

Even before he knocked, Susannah Hobson knew it was Jason Murphy standing outside her door. The sound of his boots on the steps running along the outside wall of the old house was unmistakable; the sudden spike of her pulse was par for the course.

She smoothed an unsteady hand over the long, brown hair that he had loved to see down and flowing over her bare shoulders, then made a quick scan of the living room. Like everything else in the drafty little second-floor apartment, and in spite of her best efforts, it looked like what it was—cheap, shabby and worn out.

The walls might have once been pale blue, but had long ago faded to dank, dismal gray. The springs on the sofa she'd bought last year at the secondhand store were shot, as was the floral upholstery. It had been pretty once. So had her eyes. They'd been a vibrant big-sky blue, full of hopes and dreams and the defiant pride of the very young and the very naive.

She was still young—at least in years. She was no longer naive. And although she had hopes, she had few illusions about what Jason's response would be when she broke the news. Over a month had passed since he'd climbed the creaking stairs to her apartment. He hadn't been happy that she'd tracked him down in Denver; he'd come when she'd asked him to, though, so she supposed it said something. So did the damning mix of emotions that flooded her when she opened the door and saw him standing there.

He was cowboy lanky, muscled and lean, and, along with the cold, the scent of leather and horses followed him to her door. His unusual green eyes and outlaw grin had been her undoing six months ago. She'd known then what he was. He was a circuit bronc rider; he was on the make. In spite of it— maybe even because of it—she'd still taken the tumble, just like she had half a dozen times for half a dozen guys who had all found reasons to abandon her in the past four years.

Each time, she'd hoped *this* time would be different. Each time, she'd fallen for the pretty face, the smooth lines and the promise of love everlasting. Each time, her eyes had lost a little luster and her pride had taken another hit when they'd left her.

"Hey," she said, a small kernel of hope still hovering at the fringe of reality. Maybe she'd been wrong. Maybe this cowboy would stick. "Thanks for coming."

His smile was forced and tight and as icy as the wind cutting into her apartment through the open door. "Yeah, well, you said it was important."

"Can you sit? Maybe stay for a while?"

He tucked his bare hands, scarred by his profession, chafed and red from the cold, into the hip pockets of his Wranglers. "Ah, actually, it's kind of a bad time for me."

It hurt that he wouldn't look at her. His boot tips,

caked with sludgy remnants of last night's snow, became the focal point of his attention. Susannah felt a thick, heavy acceptance settle like the lead-gray clouds scudding across the dusk sky behind his broad shoulders. They promised more cold and more snow and made her shiver. So did the closed expression on his face when he finally met her eyes. Her hope shifted, like the icy draft of the March wind, to anger.

"I'm pregnant."

She hadn't meant to blurt it out that way. And, she knew, he hadn't meant to react. She had his attention now, though. His shocked gaze narrowed on her face then dropped to her stomach. Disbelief, then grim acknowledgment, and finally anger played across the beautiful face that had hovered above hers in the dark and planted this baby inside her.

He clenched his jaw and stared behind her at some spot on the wall, then cut his gaze back to her face again. "And I suppose you're going to try to tell me it's mine." The hurtful words, like his breath, hung in the subfreezing air then drifted away with the last of her hopes.

Stung, but not really surprised, she hugged her arms around herself, suddenly so cold and so tired. "There's no 'suppose' or 'try' about it. It is yours."

He finally closed the door behind him. And stood there.

He looked as cornered as a coyote caught in the crosshairs of a rifle scope now and what had been a knee-jerk accusation transitioned to hostility—first a spark then a full-blown bonfire. There was a hole the size of a fist in her bedroom wall. The hand that had put it there curled tight at his side. He wanted to hit her. She knew he wouldn't. A cowboy had his honor.

Cowboys didn't hit women. They just knocked them up and left them to ride the next wild horse and the next wild woman. She'd watched it happen often enough to her friends and swore it would never happen to her. Now it had.

She'd never felt so alone. And alone was exactly what she hadn't wanted to be. That was why she'd called him. And until this moment, she'd thought she'd known what she wanted from him. But as he stood there looking not only trapped, but helpless and weak, she actually felt sorry for him. He was twenty-three years old, a year older than she was. She'd thought he was a man. Tonight she saw what he really was. A boy. Scared and selfish and ready to duck and run.

And she felt very old, and very alone.

"This ain't my problem," he said with a set of his jaw that dared her to deny it.

For as quiet as he'd been, he suddenly had a lot to say. It wasn't his fault; she was the one who screwed up; he wouldn't be trapped; he knew a doctor who would take care of it.

She heard the surly panic in his words like a low hum of static beneath the surprising and sudden clarity of her thoughts—thoughts that were so strong and so right, she could no longer deny them or push them to the back of her consciousness and fool herself into believing they weren't the absolute truth. She didn't want Jason Murphy, she realized as he dug into his hip pocket for his wallet, dragged out three twenties—probably all the money he had to his name—and held them out to her.

She smiled tiredly, shook her head. "I don't want your money, Jace."

He stood there, his hand extended, a defiant plea for her to take the money, assuage his guilt. "Then what do you want?"

She wanted to matter to someone. To mean something to someone. Because it was now apparent that concept would be lost on him, she didn't bother to try to explain it. "I don't want anything. I just thought you should know. Now you do. And you can go."

When she shouldered around him and opened the door, inviting him to leave the same way he'd come in, he hesitated for only a moment. He pressed the money into her hand on his way by. Then he walked out of her life without a long look back.

His tire tracks were still embedded in the snow two hours later when Susannah shrugged into her coat and boots and trudged the three blocks to the Stop and Sip where she tended bar five nights a week for minimum wage and tips. If the thought of an abortion crossed her mind during the next few months as winter grudgingly gave way to spring and the life inside her flourished and grew, it was to reject it out of hand. This baby was hers. She loved it more every day. And when, at the end of June, the morning sickness and fatigue were pretty much behind her, but the thickening of her waist made it hard to snap her jeans, she packed up her things.

It didn't take long; she didn't have much. She threw her few clothes and favorite books into the back of her ten-year-old Chevy Blazer and headed south.

There was a song that had gotten a lot of play a few years back. The lyrics came to her as drove down the highway toward the ranch where she'd grown up, where she'd been loved and which she'd left behind.

The message was about finding strength in moments of weakness. About the burden of blame and how it can trap you in the past. The song was about when it was time to move on.

Now was her time. She couldn't change the past; she could only deal with the present and hope the future held something she could handle. She wasn't going to mire herself deeper in regret and wait for the next blow to land. She was taking control of her life and making the best of it for herself and her baby.

It had taken four years of stubborn, defiant pride to reach this point. It had taken the past four months to come to terms with how she was going to do it. She had some fences to mend, but she also had someone who cared about her waiting in Colorado.

And more than anything in the world, she wanted to go home.

One

June 27, near Walden, Colorado

The sky should have been gray, leaden with clouds, heavy with rain. The day was too pretty, the sky too blue to bear witness to the carnage that lay a hundred yards below in the deep ravine.

Grim-faced, Travis Dean glanced from the destroyed metal guardrail on the narrow bridge to the skid marks and deep gouges in the dirt leading off the shoulder of the road. He made himself look at the grisly scene scarring the gorge. The knots in his stomach tightened as half-a-dozen rescue workers labored to free the occupants of the mangled vehicles. They wouldn't save any lives today. Today their gruesome task was to recover bodies.

One of them would be the body of his friend. And right now he wanted to run away from the reality of her death, as much as he'd wanted to run away from a life he'd left behind three years ago.

He made himself stay. Made himself watch in silence as the crew worked in pairs by the twisted remains of Vi Hobson's older model pickup. Several yards away, another crew labored beside the charred chassis of a vehicle that had burned to an almost unrecognizable lump of melted plastic and charred metal.

Besides his own pickup, two Jackson County Sheriff cruisers, two ambulances and a fire truck lined either side of the winding road. To his right, Chet Deerfield, Jackson County Deputy Sheriff, pulled out a notepad and pen, then pinned Trav with a squint-eyed glare. "So, how's it happen, Dean, that you were the first one to come across this, do you think?"

On Trav's left, Sheriff Del Brooks rolled his eyes at the veiled accusation in his young deputy's tone. "Oh, for God's sake, Chet, the man's ranch borders the Hobson place. Stands to reason, don't you think, that he might occasionally drive on the damn road?"

Defensive over the dressing-down, Chet puffed up his scrawny chest and pushed his wire rims back in place with the knuckle of his index finger. "Just seems a bit of a coincidence he was the one to call it in. That's all I'm saying."

"Well, if that's all you got to say, then trot your scrawny ass down the draw and see if you can help those boys with the bodies. Go on," Del ordered with a notch of his chin when Chet's jaw dropped. "Go do something useful, instead of opening your mouth and showing your ignorance."

"Damn fool," Del sputtered as Chet trudged off, then started slipping and sliding down the steep slope. "Sometimes I wonder why I ever hired him."

Travis was used to suspicious looks from Deputy Deerfield—and from most of the general populace within a fifty-mile radius of Walden, Colorado, for that matter. His grandfather may have been born and bred in the ranching community, but Trav was still considered an outsider. He was also an ex-con, a fact that didn't set right with the locals.

"He's not asking anything anyone else won't be asking before this is all over," he put in flatly.

"And you don't help matters any," Del grumbled. "In the three years since you've been here, you haven't made much effort to blend in. Yeah, yeah, I know," he added when Trav cut him a bland look. "Blendin' in's not high on your priority list. But you could do something to kill those stories that followed you from San Diego."

"And spoil everyone's fun?" Trav asked without a trace of humor.

He knew what stories Del was referring to—at least he knew the general path they took. Who knew how much they'd been embellished along the way? Someone knew someone who'd talked to someone, and, before long, word of his prison sentence had reached as far east as Walden. Not to mention speculation on the reason for it, which ranged from assault and battery to attempted murder. "Wasn't it something," they'd said, "how money talked and bought him a six-month sentence, instead of what he really deserved? Justice in the city," they'd accused, "didn't have the same teeth as frontier justice. But then, it never had."

Let 'em talk and let 'em wonder. If they were leery of him, they'd leave him alone. That was all he wanted anyway.

He met Del's eyes and thought back to those summers he used to spend here on what had then been his grandfather's ranch. They'd made friends when Trav was eight and Del was nine. While Trav had been a typical California boy—blond, tan, pencil thin and missing his surf—Del had been Opie Taylor incarnate, a freckle-faced redhead, naive and gullible. Times had changed in the thirty years since. Their friendship hadn't. Trav had grown into his shoulders and carried his one-ninety pounds—if not pieces of his past—comfortably on his six-two frame. His skin had turned the dark pecan of a man who'd spent years in the sun; his white-blond hair had gone the same way. His eyes had grown hard and cynical from the lessons he'd learned. Del, on the other hand, while still the eternal optimist, was wise to the ways of man now. At thirty-nine and with close to eighteen years of law enforcement under the size thirty-eight belt that strained to accommodate his size forty-two waist, he was no man's fool.

Despite their youthful differences, they'd connected as friends. Despite the years and the many reasons for it to be otherwise, their friendship had stood up over time. Del was still one of the few people Trav trusted. As unlikely an alliance as it had been, Vi Hobson had been another.

He set his jaw as the EMTs carefully lifted a body bag from the ground beside Vi's pickup and laid it on a stretcher.

"What the hell happened?" he ground out in frustration as he stared from her destroyed pickup to the thin wisp of smoke curling up from the other vehicle.

"That's going to take a while to sort out," Del said wearily. "Longer if we can't keep the scene clean. You said nobody's been down this road since you spotted the wreck this morning?"

"Far as I know. Can't help but wonder," Trav added, not realizing until Del jerked his head around that he'd spoken the words aloud.

"Wonder what?"

Trav rolled a shoulder. "If I'd headed over to Vi's sooner, maybe this could have been avoided."

Trav hung his hands on his hips, stared beyond the rugged terrain of the mountain ridge toward Vi's ranch, the Rocking H. "I was on my way to see her. Figured she'd be back by now."

"Back from where?"

He shook his head. "Not sure specifically. She'd taken another quick trip out east again and asked me to watch things for her. I was heading over to catch her up on what happened while she was gone." He stopped, let out a long breath. "I got this far and saw the hole in the guardrail. Then I saw the smoke rolling up out of the gorge."

Beside him, Del squinted against a summer sun that defied a cloud within a hundred miles to dim its brilliance. "Did you call it in from here or from home?"

"Here, from my cell. Then I grabbed the first-aid kit out of the toolbox and headed down."

He swallowed then sucked air hard at the memory of what he'd found when he'd gotten there.

"You'd better let someone look at that," Del said with a nod toward Trav's left arm where blood seeped through his shirtsleeve below his elbow.

Trav lifted his arm, peeled back the torn chambray and inspected the scrapes he hadn't been aware he'd gotten when he'd skidded down the gorge to get to Vi. For all the good it had done. She was already gone when he'd reached her, most likely dead on impact. And the other vehicle... The stench of burned rubber, plastic and flesh still stung his nostrils. No one could have survived that.

"Looks pretty nasty," Del added after inspecting Trav's arm.

"It's nothing," Trav said soberly. Nothing in the face of death.

Del gave him a suit-yourself shrug then walked closer to the guardrail, studying the tracks in the dirt, the skid marks on the bridge. "Plenty of speed here," he said, thinking aloud. "Doesn't figure, does it? Vi knew better than to put the pedal down on this stretch of road."

He scratched his head and resettled his uniform Stetson. "We'll pin it down eventually. Best guess—they probably both lost control. Can't figure the other car, though. Could have been at fault. See that first set of skids? Then these?" he pointed to the center of the road where tires under heavy pressure of floored brakes cut deep ruts in the dirt. "One of them appeared to be trying to get out of the other one's way and they both ended up in trouble.

"Shit," Del muttered on a defeated breath. "I hate this part of the job. There's nothing to do to help anyone."

No, Trav thought. Vi was dead. And there was nothing to do for it.

Trav distanced himself from the other mourners at the cemetery and watched Susannah Hobson. Vi's stepdaughter stood at the graveside, hollow-eyed, dressed in black. She had yet to shed a tear.

Not that he'd expected her to. He'd never met her, but everything he knew about her said she was spoiled, selfish and immature. Tears—even for a woman who had loved Susannah beyond reason—would have been too much of an effort.

"Susannah had just turned eighteen when she left four years ago," Vi had confided in Trav one day last fall when they were riding fence together. "Dale's death hit her hard. I just... Well, I always thought she'd work her anger out of her system then come back home. I never thought this much time would pass without hearing from her."

He could have told Vi then what he suspected. It was selfishness, not grief, that had kept Susannah from returning home. Most likely it was selfishness that had her trotting her little butt back here now, just in time to bury a woman who had deserved more from her. Because Vi also deserved more from him, he reconciled himself to doing what she wanted. The letter he'd received from her attorney this morning still had his mind reeling. He doubted if Susannah had had the time to even open her mail today, let alone read it.

He studied the woman's lowered head where she stood by the open wound of the freshly dug grave. The first time he'd seen Susannah's picture he'd thought she was Vi's natural daughter. He was still taken with their likeness to each other—and a little stunned by her beauty.

While Vi had worn her hair in a short, no-nonsense cut Susannah's rich, lustrous brown hair fell well below her shoulders, and was several shades lighter than Vi's. Their eyes were the same brilliant blue. Vi had been a slim five foot seven. Susannah appeared to be about the same height and equally slim. She seemed lost in her loose-fitting black dress that hung on her narrow shoulders like a sack.

It was only after he'd commented to Vi about their resemblance to each other that she'd set him straight.

"Her birth mother died when Susannah was eleven.

A rare form of cancer. She's not mine by blood and we had our problems, but I couldn't love her more if she was my own,'' Vi had said with a sadness in her voice and a faraway look in her eyes that, for some reason, had always haunted him.

What, besides Susannah, had she lost, he'd wondered at the time. Vi had had secrets; he'd never doubted it. Whenever a reference to her past before she'd married Dale Hobson a little more than ten years ago came up, she'd changed the subject. He'd respected that. Just like she'd respected his silence concerning his own past.

Trav shifted his attention back to the dry-eyed young woman. He forced himself to let up a bit. Grief took many forms. He knew that. Just like he knew the pallor in her checks came from fatigue. Same thing for the slow blink and dull glaze of her eyes. She was running on autopilot. Her movements were stiff and automated, like her body was going through the motions, but her mind had shut down.

''Amen.'' The gathered crowd echoed Pastor Dugan in a hushed murmur.

He let out a deep breath. It was done. He said a silent goodbye to his friend, then, determined to pay his respects to Susannah, walked toward the thinning knot of mourners.

He'd almost reached her when Pastor Dugan and Rachael Scott crowded in and flanked her on either side. Trav hesitated, then froze when her head came up and her gaze connected with his for the briefest of moments.

Sorrow. Aching and deep.

He was stunned by the strength of it even as he

tried not to react, tried to rein in the tug of sympathy for this beautiful young woman.

Before he could marshal his feelings, she looked away and allowed the pastor to steer her toward the waiting cars. He watched them go, then walked slowly to his pickup and, against his better judgment, followed the stream of cars to the Rocking H where the Colorado version of a wake would continue.

"How're them calves comin' along?"

Clarence Peters had sought Trav out, despite the fact that he'd isolated himself in this quiet corner of Vi's front parlor until he found an opportunity to approach Susannah. Still, he forced a smile for the arthritic old cowhand who looked up at him through rheumy eyes from beneath his gray Sunday Stetson. "They're doing fine."

As reluctant as he was to talk to anyone, Trav felt a certain empathy with the old wrangler. Clarence had been a friend of his grandfather's, a friend of Vi's. Right now he seemed as uncomfortable and as ill-equipped as Trav to handle the congestion in the wake of Vi's funeral or he'd never have approached him. No one approached Travis Dean. No one but Del and Vi.

The small room was packed with Vi's neighbors. Since the women were clustered in the kitchen, mostly men occupied the room, all of them trying not to look conspicuous about their need to get back to their spreads and the work that always waited. Violet deserved their respect, though, so they were doing their damnedest to give it, just like they were giving their all to avoid looking him in the eye.

"Dropped awful early," Clarence added, still referring to the spring calf crop, still working at small talk. He shrugged and to the overwhelming aroma of Old Spice, food wafting from the kitchen and funeral flowers, the slight movement added the faint scent of mothballs to the mix. "Guess that late snow didn't do 'em no harm."

Travis nodded, then hooked a finger beneath his collar. Damn tie had felt tight when he'd knotted it this morning. Three hours later, it was choking him, just like the small talk appeared to be choking Clarence.

"Lots of food in the kitchen. D'you get somethin' to eat?"

In these parts people said it—*it* being welcome or congratulations or, in this case, grief—with food more often than flowers. When a baby was born, someone got married or someone died, food was the commonly accepted expression of caring. And while Trav had never been the recipient of a welcome-to-the-county potluck, he knew all about the mountains of food covering the tabletop, every inch of counter space and crammed in the overflowing refrigerator.

He also knew Susannah was in the kitchen. Rather than face the group of women who surrounded her, he waited here in the packed parlor where the chatter was subdued and confined to calving, haying and the possibilities of an August drought.

"Maybe later," he said, knowing he'd pass on the food, but make himself talk to Susannah. Like it or not, he was obligated.

"Well, this is just a damn shame," Clarence said on a deep sigh, finally giving up on chitchat. "Just don't seem right that Vi's dead."

"No, it doesn't," Travis agreed, feeling the clutch of grief in his chest.

"Cain't figure out what the heck was in her head to be speeding on that road. She knew better." Clarence shook his head, talking to himself now more than to Trav. Trav let him ramble. The cause of the accident hadn't been determined, but speculation appeared to be running rampant.

"Cain't figure it at all," Clarence continued. "Unless she was trying to avoid hitting the other car. And that just leads to more questions, don't it? Been days now and I hear ain't no one claimed that other body.

"Musta been a loner," Clarence added when Trav remained silent. "Lots of loners in this world. Sad statement on the way things are these days, but there it is anyway, ain't it?"

Yeah. Trav would have to agree, even though he understood a man's need to chuck it all and walk away. It was exactly what he'd done.

Clarence shuffled his feet, then cleared his throat. "Never said this to you before." He paused, wrapped his lower lip over his upper and stared at his boot tips before continuing. "But I figure it's past time. Nothing like losing a friend to remind a person that second chances don't always come around.

"Anyway, I 'preciated the way you'd been helpin' Vi out these past three years and I been ashamed that I haven't been 'round to see ya, and, well, you know."

Yeah. Trav knew. He hadn't been around to welcome him. Neither had anyone else. That was fine. He understood. And he preferred it that way.

Clarence scratched his ear then tugged on his hat brim. "Don't know if she told you, but I was the

Hobson foreman for eighteen years. When Dale up and died four years ago, right after I'd retired, well, I was real worried about Vi. Real worried 'bout whether she could keep on keepin' on by herself out here."

The old man squinted up into Trav's eyes and nodded once, as if grudgingly admitting to himself that he liked what he saw. "You done right by her, boy. What with little Susannah flying the coop right after her daddy died well, that left Vi in a fix. That first year by herself was rough on her."

Clarence's endorsement surprised him. He managed a smile. "I don't think there was ever any question about who was really helping who."

Clarence chuckled softly. "Well, yeah, she told me you was as green as a new shoot when you hit the scene. But I reckon even then you was helping each other some. And your back was a might lot stronger than hers. I always figured that's what made the difference between her hangin' on or sellin' out."

His back had been about all he'd had to offer that first year. That and his veterinary experience, which had come in damn handy even if he was out of practice and his specialty had been in small animals.

"Somethin' else needs to be said," Clarence added after a moment. "I'm glad you didn't let your granddaddy's spread get bought out by that blasted development company, neither. Charlie Dean and me go way back. Rode a lotta trail and ate a lotta dust together. It pained him when your daddy and his brothers went off to college and never came back. He never said as much 'cause he'd never been one to hold no one back, but he'd always hoped one of 'em would want to carry on."

The life wasn't for everyone, Trav thought in defense of his father and his uncles who had opted out of the often grueling and generally shoestring operations of a Colorado cattle ranch, but he didn't say as much. While he'd enjoyed his summer visits to the Lazy D when he was a kid, Trav hadn't seen ranching in his future, either. Not back then. Back then—hell, as recently as three years ago—he hadn't seen a lot of things, he thought grimly.

When Charlie and Treva retired to Arizona where the warm, dry weather eased their arthritis if not the occasional pangs of homesickness for Colorado and the Lazy D, Travis had seen it as the perfect place to hide out, lick his wounds. His practice was gone, and so was his wife. So now, instead of the fat portfolio he'd been building, he had a prison record and a mortgage the size of the Rockies. Not to mention a back that ached every night. Such was the price of solitude.

"You've done him proud," Clarence continued, snapping Trav away from the memories he avoided thinking about at all costs and usually managed to avoid. "It ain't none of my business what happened before you come here, but I know you had your troubles. Charlie must be pleased to see what you've done with the Lazy D."

Trav would always regret how his *troubles* had spilled over into his parents' and his grandparents' lives. It had been hard on them. In some way, he supposed he viewed taking over the Lazy D and keeping it in the family as atonement for what he'd put them through.

"This house," Clarence continued, changing direction when several moments passed, "this house has seen too much death, you ask me. First Dale four years ago—and his first wife, Mae, long before that. Now Vi. Just don't seem right. And now that poor little girl is left with no one.''

He glanced toward the kitchen, knowing he'd put off talking to her long enough. He had more to offer Susannah than his condolences, but what he had to tell her wasn't going to be easy for either of them.

"I've got to be moving on home," he said, surprising himself by giving the old man an affectionate clasp on the shoulder. "I'll just go pay my respects to Susannah and be on my way."

"You make sure you say hey to my Martha on your way out the door. Better wrap up a piece or two of her fried chicken for supper while yer at it. Best around." His eyes twinkled. "You'll be sorry if you don't."

"Tell you what," Trav said, and found he couldn't stall a grin, "you eat an extra piece for me, then you can gloat all night about what I missed out on."

Clarence was still chuckling and Trav was still smiling at the unexpected warmth in the old man's eyes as he walked away. He sobered when his gaze snagged on Susannah. She was making her way through the kitchen door and into the dining room, sandwiched again between Pastor Dugan and Rachael Scott who seemed to have made it their personal mission to shore her up.

He stopped, watched her in grim silence as, one by one, Vi's neighbors lined up to relay their final condolences and say their goodbyes.

When the pastor and Rachael finally drifted off in other directions, leaving her alone, he decided to get it over with. Jaw set, he walked up to her—only to have her turn back into the kitchen before he got to

her. He hesitated, then followed, pausing at the
kitchen door as she filled a plate with chicken and
roast beef and a thick slab of ham. Then she drifted
outside, unnoticed by anyone but him.

The chattering women grew quiet suddenly when
they spotted him, then made a big show of tidying up
as he entered the kitchen. Eyes dead ahead, he continued on through the room, leaving the house
through the back door. Whether he wanted to or not,
he was determined to speak with Susannah before he
left, no matter how many pairs of eyes followed him
in disapproving silence.

Two

She could have been a statue, she sat so still on the bottom porch step. Her low croons and the soft slide of her hair spilling over her left shoulder stopped Trav with his hand on the screen door. He held it open so as not to startle her. At least that was what he told himself when, in fact, he was the one who was startled by the picture she made sitting there.

Her head was down; her cheek rested on her knees, which she'd pulled to her chest. Beside her feet lay Vi's black-and-white border collie, Sooner, her narrow nose wedged in abject misery between her paws. The plate of food sat untouched on the ground beside her feet.

"I know you miss her, girl, but you've got to eat," she coaxed softly as she stroked the collie's head with a gentle touch of her fingertips. "It's not good for you. It's not what Vi would have wanted. Poor girl. Poor pretty girl. Won't you eat something today? Please."

Trav let out a long breath, then eased the door shut behind him. He'd left food for the collie in the barn every day when he breezed in, did chores and breezed out again, making it a point *not* to stop at the house and introduce himself. He hadn't been surprised when the collie's food had pretty much gone untouched for the first couple of days after Vi's death. He hadn't, however, expected the dog to grieve this long or this deeply.

"She still not eating?" He walked across the porch and down the steps to hunker down by Sooner's side.

Susannah glanced up at him then back to the dog, more concerned about the collie's condition than the fact that she didn't know him. "I've tried everything. If this banquet doesn't coax her into eating, I don't know what it's going to take."

Trav skimmed his hands over Sooner's back and ribs. The corners of his mouth turned down when he felt the weight loss. He pressed his palm against her belly, held it there.

"She's bloated, isn't she?" she asked gravely.

"What she is, is pregnant," he said and felt a small amount of relief when he felt movement against his palm.

"Pregnant?" She glanced from him to Sooner, a look of such deep, heartfelt empathy crossing her face that he had to look away.

"Due in two or three weeks. The pups are doing okay," he said as he moved his hands to Sooner's head, stroked her muzzle. "There's a good girl. You're okay now, aren't you?" he murmured, peeling back her lip and checking her gums for color. She was holding on, but this couldn't continue much longer.

"Are you a vet?"

He stood, his eyes returning to Sooner because it was easier than looking at the pale, concerned woman who had somehow managed to make him want to reassure her when he damn well knew better than to even like her too much.

"Travis Dean," he said rather than answer her.

She stood then too and extended her hand. He hesitated for a moment before grasping it. It was very small, that hand. Very small, very cold and whatever strength it might have had appeared to have been leeched away hours ago by fatigue.

"Susannah Hobson." Her voice, like her eyes, was void of any real presence or curiosity.

"My condolences on your loss," he said, fighting yet another unexpected tug of sympathy for this young woman whose hand felt so fragile in his.

He wasn't sure who was responsible for prolonging the contact. It could have been him; he was half afraid she'd keel over if he let go. Or it could have been her, because he represented something warm and solid to hang onto in the cold aftermath of death and her concern for the dog.

"Thank you," she said. "And thank you for coming."

He wondered how many times she'd delivered the same sentiment today, then tamped down another small pang of sympathy that tried to work its way into his awareness.

He could have left then. He'd done his duty. He'd paid his respects. He could call her tomorrow and hit her with the news that had hit him just this morning. But everything about her seemed so fragile. And her eyes were so lost and weary and so old for someone so young. Whether her pain came from guilt or grief, both of which were too little, too late in his opinion, she was suffering. And she had been loved by his friend.

"I've got something to help get her over the hump." He nodded toward the listless dog and suddenly aware that he still held her hand in his, released it. "It's a nutritional supplement. Comes in paste form. You just squirt it into her mouth a couple of times a day. It should prevent dehydration and bolster her diet enough to keep her going until she decides to eat again."

She turned worried eyes to the dog. "How long do you think that will be?"

He shrugged. "It's hard to tell. I wouldn't think much longer."

"She misses her."

"Yeah. So do I."

She looked up at him then. Guilt blended with what could have been curiosity or simply the need to take her mind off of Sooner's misery. "Should I know you?"

When those big blue eyes fastened on his, he found himself captivated by not only the intensity of the color, but by the strength that fought off the fatigue of what had to have been a grueling day.

"Charlie and Treva Dean are my grandparents."

She was slow to put it together, but she finally nodded. "The Lazy D. Yes, of course. How is Charlie? And Treva?" she added, digging deep to connect with a conversation she very clearly had little energy to handle.

"Good. They're good," he repeated, hooking a boot on the lowest step and crossing his arms over his chest, distancing himself physically. "They're retired now. Moved to Arizona three years ago."

When she merely nodded, he decided she hadn't been back long enough to hear the stories about him or she'd be running for the house and the protection it offered. It also confirmed his earlier conclusion that she hadn't yet read her mail and the letter from Vi's attorney.

Since she hadn't run, he felt another compulsion to fill the silence. "I got to know Vi pretty well these past few years since I took over the Lazy D. I was proud to call her my friend."

It was an understatement as well as a surprise to both him and to Vi that they'd become friends at all. Just as the news he'd received from her attorney in the mail this morning had been a surprise. More like a shock—one he still hadn't recovered from. Susannah may never recover from it.

Though Vi had played most of her cards close to the vest, he'd never doubted her devotion to Susannah—although he wasn't sure Susannah would see it that way when the full repercussions of Vi's will set in. Vi had spoken of the girl often with love and understanding despite the heartache Susannah had caused her by running away. It was rough when a kid ran, but Trav had been around long enough to know it took two to tango. This one had at least come home even if it was too late. That didn't mean he wouldn't do as right by her as he could, given the conditions of Vi's will.

"I know this has hit you hard. I also know you haven't had a chance to even think about the stock or much of anything else for that matter."

A sudden awareness replaced the distant attention in her eyes. "Mr. Dean, oh, I'm sorry. It just registered. You're the neighbor. The one the pastor told me is taking care of things. I'm so sorry," she repeated. "I'd meant to contact you before now. To thank you for everything you've done. Everything you're doing."

"It's not a problem. And it's not anything Vi wouldn't have done for me."

"Yes, but I'm not Vi. And you don't even know me."

No. She wasn't Vi. Vi had been sixty if she'd been a day and she'd had all the time and careworn weathering of anyone who'd spent that many years working the range. Susannah looked like a babe in the woods, tired, yes, but with the resiliency of youth to support her.

She was in her twenties and he was guessing early twenties at that. Great. He kept himself from letting out a weary sigh. A twenty-something orphan with a ranch to run was the last damn thing he needed hanging around his neck.

"Look...I know you've pretty much been bombarded with the funeral and all the details that went with it since you've been back." He paused when a mist of tears gathered in her eyes and fought a reluctant stirring of respect when she forcefully blinked them back. He cleared his throat. "I need to touch base with you on a few things."

The blue eyes turning to his were confused.

He considered hitting her with it then, but it would be like kicking someone when they were down. He'd never been big on sucker punches. He wasn't going to start throwing them now.

"Tomorrow will be soon enough, if you're up to it," he said. "I'll be over in the morning to do chores. We can talk then."

"Tomorrow." She closed her eyes, as if tomorrow was as far away as next year and it was all she could do to get through today. "All right," she said. "We can talk tomorrow."

She gave Sooner one final concerned pat on the head and turned back toward the house. "If you'll excuse me, I need to have another word with Pastor Dugan before he leaves."

He watched her through the screen door as she made her way through the thinning group of mourners who took her hand or gave her a hug as she passed them by.

Tomorrow, after she'd had a little more time to grieve, he'd lay it all out, make her see reason, make her see sense. And with a little luck, a couple of weeks from now she'd be gone.

Later that afternoon when the house was quiet and the sun was about to set and she and Sooner were alone in the kitchen, Susannah's thoughts drifted back to Travis Dean. He'd been good with the dog, kind to search her out and deliver his condolences, kind in the way so many of the hometown folks had been these last couple of days. Awful days.

Sitting on the kitchen floor, the cupboards at her back, another plate of food at her side and Sooner's long, soft muzzle resting on her thigh, she told herself he was right about one thing. Tomorrow would be soon enough to deal with whatever it was he wanted to talk to her about.

She was exhausted. For what was left of the day, she didn't want to think at all. Not about him. Not about tomorrow. She just wanted Sooner to eat.

"Come on, sweetie," she coaxed softly. "If I can do it, you can do it."

For the baby's sake, she forced down another bite of the roast beef and cheese sandwich she'd made. She tore off a corner and offered it to Sooner. The collie lifted her head, sniffed, then lowered her muzzle to Susannah's lap again.

"Don't die."

The unexpected fear in her trembling whisper broke into the total silence and unleashed a flood of pent-up emotions. She tried desperately to catch them up, swallow them back, to maintain the control that had gotten her through the last four months and the last three days. But the sound of her own voice in the too, too silent kitchen—plaintive, hopeless, riding on the edge of panic—frightened her. And once one emotion broke through, the others funneled in through the gaping hole.

"Please, Sooner. Please...please don't you die, too."

The last word broke on a sob. With the cold, hard tile beneath her, the tentative warmth of the collie beside her and the tick of the battery-powered clock hanging above the kitchen sink her only witness, she finally let herself cry.

She cried for Sooner and her puppies. She cried for Vi, whom she'd come home to see only to find her gone. She cried for her father who had died too soon and her mother who had died too young. She cried for her own baby who would grow up without a father. She even cried for Jason Murphy who was so selfish and so stupid to throw away his chance at being a part of this miracle growing inside her.

When Sooner nuzzled her wet nose to Susannah's cheek, her liquid brown eyes doleful and filled with sorrow, Susannah wrapped her arms around the dog's silky warmth. And finally she cried for herself.

She'd come home to start a new life and mend fences with Vi. She'd come home too late.

* * *

Dry-eyed finally, head pounding, Susannah pressed a cold cloth to her eyes and watched, mildly encouraged as Sooner drank a little of the milk she'd poured into a saucer and set on the floor. She didn't drink much, but it was something and it gave Susannah hope.

"Go to bed," she ordered herself aloud. It was where she needed to be. But she was beyond exhaustion. Too tired to sleep, too edgy and restless to read, she wandered into the den. There were so many things in this room that were familiar. The old tweed sofa, with its sprung frame and worn cushions, was still covered by the wedding ring quilt her grandmother Jacobs had made. The aerial photograph of the homestead, matted and framed, still hung on the wall to the right of the bookcase. The curtains were new. So was the computer, relatively speaking. It was something her dad had never wanted anything to do with.

"If it doesn't have a dial, I've got no use for it," her dad used to say. The memory made her smile. Vi used to get so put out with him and his stubborn ways that kept him mired in the age of dial phones, eight-track tapes and a certain style of Wranglers that Les, down at the hardware store, had to order in special just for him.

There had been a sweetness to his steadfast grip on the old ways. Vi had indulged him even if she hadn't approved. Once he was gone, however, it looked like she'd updated a few things, starting with the computer.

Susannah sat down at the desk and glanced briefly at the stack of unopened mail. Bills, newspapers, an envelope from a law office. She wasn't up to dealing with any of it now. Instead, she turned on the computer. If nothing else, noodling around with it might take her mind off Sooner and her neighbor, Travis Dean. Why she kept thinking about him, she wasn't sure. Mixed signals maybe. Cool blue eyes and offers of help. Maybe he wanted out from under. Maybe that was what he wanted to talk to her about tomorrow. It had to be a drain for him, taking care of his spread and hers, too.

She wondered if he had a family. He was an attractive man. Stood to reason he probably had a wife, maybe some kids. She shook her head, prodding herself away from thoughts of him. She needed to be thinking about what she was going to do now, not about her blond neighbor with the brooding eyes. She needed to get a feel for how things stood financially. Yesterday, before the visitation, she'd thumbed through the file cabinets. The absence of any recent written records told her Vi must have converted the books to the computer.

If so and if she could figure out the software program, Susannah could get a feel for the finances. She wanted to stay here. She wanted to raise her baby here. She owed it to herself. She owed it to Vi. To do that, she had to get her finger on the pulse of the operation as it was today.

The monitor lit up. ENTER PASSWORD blinked at her. She sagged back in the chair. She hadn't anticipated Vi would have her entry password protected. Now what?

"Nothing to do, but try."

And she did try. She tried Vi, Violet, Hobson, Dale, Sooner. She tried the horses' names, birth dates, days of the week, months, and was about to give up when she decided to try her own name, just for the heck of it.

"Bingo."

She felt a clutch of guilt and grief to think Vi had used even this small way to keep in touch with her as the icons popped up and cluttered the desktop. Since she wasn't sure what she was searching for, she started with the Documents icon and found a dozen or so files, none of which appeared to be ranch records. One file, however, caught her eye and for some reason, had her heart skipping a beat.

She stared at the file name: Secrets

A long-lost and pleasant memory surfaced. It had been a year after her mom had died, the winter after her father had married Vi—a long and particularly hard winter. Vi had invented a game for the two of them to play to relieve the boredom. She'd found a string of secret hiding places around the house and ranch and would hide little treasures for Susannah to search for and find when she grew bored and restless.

Violet had made sure she had items on hand for those long winter days—a favorite candy bar, a cookie, a book, sometimes a new dress for Susannah's favorite doll—and had hidden the little treasures in a dozen odd nooks and crannies.

Susannah thought back and remembered a secret panel below the bottom step leading to the attic, another behind a loose stone by the storm-cellar door. There were many others, most of which she had since forgotten. Vi's game would keep her busy for hours, searching for buried treasure.

Vi had tried so hard. "And you were so stingy with your affections," she said to herself aloud, remembering, feeling a renewed sting of guilt. She'd been twelve. She gave herself that. She'd been hurting for her mother. Vi had known and she'd been patient beyond belief.

Wishing things had been different, wishing she'd come home long before now, Susannah clicked on the Secrets file. Several notations, ranging from reminders to change the water filter to pay quarterly taxes, all appeared routine. One single notation seemed to be yet another generic entry: "Buy mortar for the loose stone."

She moved on past it, then backed up and read it again. Her heart skipped then double pumped; all of her instincts flipped into overdrive. *Buy mortar for the loose stone.*

She sat back in the chair, staring at the screen. It had been a standing joke between them. If she'd gotten into mischief and Violet wanted to hold a threat over her head, she'd laughingly say, "You'd better watch yourself, missy, or I'll mortar up that loose stone in the storm cellar wall and you'll never find a treasure there again." They'd both known Violet would never reset the stone; it held too many memories and too much sentiment.

She shifted her gaze from the screen to the window and beyond, where the day had turned to night without her realizing it. Beneath a full moon, she could make out the shadow of the grass-covered dome of the storm cellar.

The cellar had been there forever. Double wooden doors lay at a forty-five-degree angle to its entrance, protecting the opening. The steps and walls leading down into the earth were made of stone and mortar and shored up the manmade cave that had been used over the years to keep vegetables and fruits cool in the summer and from freezing during the winter. And a time or two, she could remember huddling there against her mother's side, a candle their only light as the wind screamed above them, rain and hail pelting the doors when a particularly nasty spring storm had cut a vicious path through the valley.

Buy mortar for the loose stone.

The entry seemed so innocuous and yet she couldn't shake the notion that it seemed like... Could it possibly be? Somehow it seemed like a message.

It was crazy. It was also compelling. So much so that every instinct she owned called out to her. *Check it out. Don't just sit here.*

"Come on, girl." She coaxed Sooner to her feet as she rose, found a flashlight in the kitchen then walked outside. Just as she stepped off the porch, a slow-moving cloud covered the moon. The night turned black as pitch.

For the most part, she'd been on her own for the past four years. She was used to solitude. But there was an aloneness in this night that could not compare with any other. Especially now, as she walked across the dew-damp grass in the yard of the one place she had always known love and had never truly been by herself.

She was by herself tonight. And she'd never felt the loss of her family more. Shaking off the loneliness as well as a niggling and unsettling sense of unease, she approached the storm cellar doors. For a long moment, she simply stood before them, staring at the weathered wooden planks as the beam of the flashlight shined on the latch.

Buy mortar for the loose stone.

On a deep breath, she flicked open the heavy hook

latch, then tugged one of the doors up and open. To the sounds of crickets and a gentle wind rattling the aspen, the eerie complaint of rusted hinges groaned into the night.

If true dark had a scent, it was what rose on the sleeping draft of stagnant air pushing up from the black depths of the cave. It smelled exactly as she remembered. Musty and cool and dank.

A little frisson of unease, the kind that hovered at the edge of consciousness and instinctively warned her away from murky, foreign places, rode on a breath of awareness. It warned of things that went bump in the night and dragged along childhood memories of creatures that scrabbled in the dark.

She drew a steadying breath and, balancing with one hand on the side of the double door that remained in place, shined the light down the uneven steps. A ripple of dread washed down her spine, standing the hair at her nape on end as she contemplated walking down into the unknown awaiting her.

"This is stupid," she berated herself then made herself take two downward steps. "There's nothing in here, but air and maybe a few toads…or a spider or two and…maybe a snake. You know what, Sooner? This could probably wait until tomorrow morning. It's a wild goose chase anyway. I mean, really. Talk about a vivid imagination."

Just then her beam of light flashed on the wall of stone—and recognition snapped back like a rubber band. Her memories tugged back into place when a single stone caught her eye. It was the one. The one Vi used to hide the most precious treasures behind. Spotting it, she knew she'd never sleep a wink tonight if she didn't see this through.

With a sense of now-or-never, she descended three more steps until she could reach it. The first thing she noticed was that the stones around it were covered with a fine film of dust. The loose stone wasn't, as if it had recently been handled.

Again, her heart slammed her a couple of times in the chest, but she reached for the stone, grasped and tugged. It was cold and heavy as it scraped stubbornly against earth and surrounding rock and finally slid free. She set it on the step above her, then shined the flashlight beam into the hole where the stone had been. Her breath backed up in her throat, stalled in her chest and thickened.

The light glinted across something that was not earth nor mortar nor rock. Something gleaming white under the concentrated light. With trembling fingers, she reached in and pulled it out. Then, with a sense of shock and disbelief, she stared at the bulging white envelope lying in her hand.

She recognized Vi's handwriting as the beam of her flashlight revealed one single word. Scrawled across the front of the envelope was her name: SUSANNAH.

Three

Susannah didn't remember climbing back out of the cellar. She didn't remember closing the door, latching it and walking back to the house with the envelope clutched to her breast. As she sat in the dimly lit kitchen with the light above the sink casting shadows over the old oak table and held the contents of the envelope in her hands, it was all she could do to remember to breathe.

She stared at the delicate gold chain draped across her palm. The chain had been cold when she'd pulled it out of the envelope. So had the pair of gold-and-ruby rings. They were warm now. She'd clutched them so tightly in her fist they'd taken on her body heat, which was amazing, since she felt icy with shock and confusion, wondering what it all meant.

There was no question; they were Vi's rings. The ones she'd always worn on this same chain around her neck. Susannah had never seen her without them and was certain that in all the time she'd known her, Vi had never taken them off. Both were wide gold bands. Both were encrusted with a single large round ruby. One, judging from the size, was a man's ring; the other was unmistakably a woman's.

"Can I wear them?" she remembered asking Vi once. "They're so pretty."

"They are pretty, aren't they, sweetie? And they're

very special to me. If I'd ever want anyone to wear them, it would be you. But I made a promise to someone to never take them off. You can look and touch all you want, though, okay?''

Tears filled her eyes as she held the rings and the chain over the top of the old oak table. What could have compelled Vi to take them off? And why on earth had she tucked them in this envelope and then hidden them in the storm cellar where they might never have been found?

She stared from the rings to the envelope and felt a sinking sensation as if she was plummeting into a mystery that was surreal and abstract and a little frightening. Also inside the envelope, in addition to the rings, was a sheet of paper. Like the envelope, her name was written at the top. But below her name, Vi had written a series of numbers—several lines of them. At first glance, it had made absolutely no sense. She frowned at the seemingly haphazard arrangement of numbers, then realized with a catch in her chest, what she was actually seeing. Code.

Her heart kicked up again, like a rabbit running scared from some unknown threat, some unknown enemy. Vi had written something in code. The implications were too numerous to digest. She thought back to those long cold winters again.

Like the secret hiding places, Vi had made up another game to help pass the time. She'd invented a code with which they would write each other notes. Susannah used to spend hours lost in the fun task of breaking it.

She knew she was looking at that same code now. On wobbly legs, she rose. With trembling fingers, she grabbed a pencil from a mug on the counter. Then lost in concentration, she sat down and began the task of deciphering it.

It surprised her how fast it came back to her, considering her fingers were tingling with nervous anticipation and her mind was staggered by each word she untangled. She had a few false starts, but eventually fell into the rhythm. Vi had reversed the alphabet, numbered the letters from one to twenty-six then transposed every fifth set of letters. It was a simple code, designed for the pleasure of a twelve-year-old girl, but still, it took almost half an hour to translate the short message. And what she finally read sent her mind reeling.

Susannah, my sweet girl. I must make this short as time is running out. The existence of this letter must seem strange to you. Stranger still is the notion that you will actually find it where I've hidden it in the storm cellar. But life, I've found, is strange, most of it a complete mystery. I have felt compelled these past months to find you. I've sensed even that you may be in the process of finding your own way home again. I do so hope it's true for it means you may have actually found this message. You always were a clever girl.

You couldn't know, but I've lived on the edge of fate my entire life. Now fate is warning me to leave Colorado, to leave the country for someplace where I will be safe. Safe from what, I cannot tell you, as that knowledge could place you in jeopardy, as well, and I would do anything to keep you from harm. I must believe all will be well just as you must believe that I understand why you left and why you stayed away.

In the meantime, treasure always what we shared, as I do. Remember always the treasure that is life. I so hope to be in contact with you soon.

My love, Violet.

Shaken, Susannah reread the letter that had left her both shocked and confused. Vi's forgiveness made her heart ache. And her vague references to jeopardy and warnings and fate—what did it all mean? Fate had told Vi to leave the country? To be safe? Safe from what? Safe from whom? And why would she be in danger? Why, also, had she signed it Violet? She'd never, in all the time Susannah had known her, gone by anything, but Vi.

She stared at the deciphered letter, then beyond it, into the silence of the kitchen. Why had Vi hidden the message when the chances of it being found were almost nil? "And why did you write it in code? A code only I could understand?"

The clock above the sink showed ten-thirty-five. As the hands ticked their way toward eleven o'clock, possible answers to those particular questions began to form. Vi had anticipated something terrible was about to happen. Her hope had been that if anyone found the message, it would only be someone who would understand the clue she'd left on the computer and would know to look in the storm cellar. Only someone who could decipher the code.

"She didn't want anyone to be able to find this or anyone to read this but me," she murmured aloud. "Because she knew she was in danger. Now she's dead."

Her hushed whisper crept into the hollow silence of the room like a warning that had arrived too late. She heard her heart beat in her ears as she stared from the letter to the gold rings still clutched in her hand. The same unassailable sense of foreboding that had hit her when she'd returned home and found Vi dead gripped her now. The general speculation was Vi's death had been an accident, although the official investigation hadn't yet been completed.

This note implied otherwise. This note implied it wasn't an accident. That someone had killed Vi.

The wave of incredulity swamping her was dizzying. "My God."

She rose, clutching her arms around herself to ward off a sudden chill. Could it be? Could it possibly be?

But why? Why would someone want Vi dead? It didn't make any sense. In her message, she'd said she was going to leave the country, go somewhere she would be safe. "Safe from something she couldn't tell me about because it might place me in danger, too."

If Susannah was to believe any of this, then should she believe she was in danger now? Along with the disbelief and the doubts and the possibility any of this could be credible, that question had been prowling the edge of her consciousness ever since she'd decoded the message. And fear, like breath, became a basic part of her existence.

The night beyond the kitchen window was completely dark now. A heavy layer of clouds folded in on each other and covered the dome of night sky. As she stood there, never more aware of the darkness and her vulnerability, for the first time in her life she truly understood fear. If Vi had been in danger, is this the way she'd felt before she died?

Silence, as heavy as the air in the cave, closed in around her. She was alone. Miles from the nearest neighbor. Completely defenseless against an attack. Was there still a gun in the house? Did she have need of one?

She thought of the child sleeping inside her, a child who deserved to grow strong and experience life. She placed a protective hand across her middle. Propelled by a sudden surge of panic, she ran to the den, wrenched open the closet door. She dug frantically through clothes and boxes, searching for the old rifle she remembered her dad kept there to scare off coyotes. Relief sighed through her in a rushing wave when she found it—rusted and heavy, deadly and cold. A little more digging and she found a box of bullets.

She stopped, stared at the weapon in her hand. She knew how to use it. You didn't grow up on a remote ranch and not know how to defend cattle from predators.

The question was: Did she need it to defend herself? Could she use it to defend herself? The idea of actually firing at a human being sent a jolt of nausea roiling through her system.

"Stop." She drew a steadying breath, forced reason. "Think. You're overreacting."

She'd been here by herself for four nights now. She'd been alone all that time. Surely, if she were in any danger, if someone intended to come after her, they'd have done so by now. Then another thought occurred to her. Maybe that someone was dead. They'd yet to identify the person who had died in the same crash that had killed Vi. Maybe the threat died with them.

And maybe there was no threat at all. She dragged a hand through her hair, realized how utterly exhausted she was. She wasn't thinking straight. And why should she be? She'd been gone four years; she'd returned expecting to renew and repair her relationship with Vi only to find her dead. This morning she'd buried the one person left on this earth who had loved her.

Drawing a calming breath for the baby's sake as much as her own, she walked back to the kitchen as another thought occurred to her. She reread the message. Aside from the cryptic tone and the vague sense of danger, something else about it had bothered her. It finally registered what it was: The date was missing. It was impossible to tell from the content when Vi had written the note. Was it recently? Or had it been years ago, possibly three or four, when Vi had been feeling lonely and bruised and maybe even a little confused herself?

She'd just lost her husband. Susannah had left her, as well. Maybe…maybe she'd snapped a little. Maybe she'd been depleted, drowning in her own grief. Maybe it had been Vi's way of reaching out, of attempting to reconnect with something.

"And maybe you'd best go to bed then look at things again tomorrow in the light of day."

She picked up the chain holding the rings. Slowly, she slipped it over her head. The weight of the gold between her breasts and the connection with Vi felt somehow comforting. She folded the note and, gripping it in her hand, walked to the door and locked it.

The coded message she tucked in her dresser

drawer beneath her underwear in her old bedroom under the stairs. It haunted her as she lay in her double bed, worrying the gold bands between her fingers. The rifle she'd loaded and placed on the floor under the bed gave her little sense of peace. Nothing did.

Where just yesterday she'd found solace in this room, she now found uncertainty. Where the sounds of the old house settling had just last night felt familiar and friendly, tonight each unexpected noise had her eyes flying open and her pulse rate spiking.

She finally fell into a fitful sleep. What time, she didn't know. And she dreamed. Of fiery car crashes and a woman's screams. Of unknown killers burned beyond recognition. Of sunlight glinting off blood-red rubies and fourteen-karat gold, coded messages hidden in the deep dank dark. She dreamed of the horses in the barn and Sooner who sat in front of a bowl of food and refused to eat.

Don't die. Don't die.

The gentle swell of movement inside her belly finally soothed her. Life. She'd just begun to feel it this past week. Little quickenings that made tears of wonder well in her eyes. She rolled to her side, caressed the slight, hard mound of her abdomen and marveled as her baby tumbled.

"Hush, hush. Go to sleep," she murmured, and, comforted by the strong new heart that beat inside her, she finally drifted into oblivion.

Willard Croft sat in the shadows behind his desk at the Coalition compound in Oregon. The former CIA agent propped his elbows on his ink blotter and steepled his hands in front of his mouth. He glared at the phone, absently tapping his index fingers to his lips. He was not a patient man. And he didn't like being kept in the dark. Contact from the man assigned to shadow Violet Vaughn was four days overdue. And now the operative he'd sent to Colorado to report on both their man's and Violet's status was an hour late checking in.

He despised waiting. Despised ineptitude even more. This was beginning to show all the markings of a bungled mess.

When the phone finally rang at 1:17 a.m., he snatched up the receiver on the first ring. He said nothing. The operative on the other end of the line with access to his private number knew what information was required.

"The woman is no longer an issue," the voice, void of emotion, stated flatly.

Croft expelled a seething breath. Killing Violet Vaughn had not been part of the plan. The others, especially Agnes and Oliver, would not be pleased to hear this. "How?"

"According to the local paper, she drove off a mountain road and into a ravine four days ago. It appears to have been an 'accident.'"

Croft dragged a hand over his face while his blood pressure rose sharply. "Witnesses?"

"None."

The small measure of relief that piece of good news brought helped him gather his composure. "And our man?"

"Went the same way, at the same time."

The crude expletive he uttered pierced the stillness of the room like a lance. The inept fool. Whatever information he may have pried out of Violet about Code Proteus had died with him.

Despite his rage he had to keep a clear head. "All right. Are there any untidy details we need to be concerned about?"

"Not that I've seen. Our guy is nothing but cinders. They'll never ID him. Within a year, the local Barneys will forget all about him when no one claims what's left of the body."

Croft felt no remorse over the loss of the Coalition's muscle man. What he felt was a teeming anger over the missed opportunity. Violet Vaughn was their link to Code Proteus. She was also their best lead to her five genetically engineered children who had been presumed dead until the World Bank heist occurred several months ago. That job had done more than wreak universal economic fallout: it had brought to light that at least two of them were alive. If there were two, then it was possible the others were also alive. If so, the Coalition wanted to know about them. Violet Vaughn may have been the key.

The last communication he'd had with the now-dead operative had been several days ago when he'd called to report that he was closing in on Violet in Colorado. She'd just left the interstate heading for the mountains. When he'd received no further contact, it was decided to dispatch a second operative to investigate. Now he knew why he'd never reported back. Dead men don't make reports.

And the dead woman...well, he had wanted Violet Vaughn alive for what she could have told them about the five genetically engineered subjects. If nothing else, he would have used her for bait to draw them out of hiding. She was, after all, their mother.

"What else do I need to know?"

"There's a stepdaughter on the scene. She's been out of the picture for several years, though."

"And now?"

"Now she's back, but clueless. I'll stake my reputation that Susannah Hobson knows nothing. And there's nothing in the house, either. I took the liberty of completing a thorough search during the funeral services."

It was on the tip of Croft's tongue to issue orders to eliminate the stepdaughter. But then, was it really necessary? He stroked his index finger over his upper lip. Violet Vaughn hadn't managed to keep herself and her five children hidden and presumed dead for over twenty years by being careless. If she hadn't taken the initiative to contact Jake Ingram, one of her firstborn, the Coalition would have had no idea she was still alive. And then, of course, if Ingram's name hadn't appeared in every newspaper in the country when he'd gotten called in to help solve the World Bank robbery, they never would have put two and two together.

Yes. Violet had kept her secrets well. She wouldn't have told the stepdaughter anything, and killing her on the remote chance she did know something would only draw attention to the Coalition. One unexplained accident was plausible. Two slid beyond plausible to suspicious.

He made his decision. "Pull out of there," he ordered. "If it becomes necessary, we'll deal with her later."

For a long time after he hung up, he sat in the dark, debating how to break the news of Violet Vaughn's death to the rest of the Coalition. They weren't going to like this. They weren't going to like this at all.

Trav had done his chores, saddled Max, his five-year-old sorrel gelding, and was heading for the Hobson place by seven the next morning on a day that had dawned sunny and bright. It was an hour horseback ride. It would have taken twenty minutes in his truck, but he'd wanted to ride this morning. Wanted to clear his head, flesh out his arguments, work on his patience. And Boomer needed the exercise.

He glanced at the silver and white mini-schnauzer bouncing along ahead of him through the new grass, sniffing out rabbit warrens and snapping at flies, and shook his head. As a working dog, Boomer was a joke and an embarrassment. As company, he was demanding and opinionated and totally without manners. He was also a leftover from San Diego and in the end Travis had felt sorry for the little rat and dragged him along to Colorado.

His jaw was tightly clenched when he crested the ridge and pulled himself away from his past best forgotten and, more important, over. The present was what lay before him—the Hobson homestead. It looked like a brush-and-oil painting of verdant greens and fertile earth against the breathtaking backdrop of the pine-forested mountains. Lying at their feet like velvet pillows, the foothills, still heavy with grass, were dotted with placidly grazing cattle. This had been Hobson land for over a hundred years. For that reason alone, he considered reining in and heading back home without breaking the news to Susannah.

But he tugged his hat lower over his brow and kneed the gelding into a brisk jog-trot, more determined than ever to see this through. He couldn't put this off any longer just because Susannah Hobson wasn't going to like the taste of the news he was going to feed her—although he figured the dollar signs punctuating his message would go a long way to soothe her anger over the parts she didn't find palatable.

For the first time since he'd heard from Vi's attorney, he let himself assess the Rocking H through different eyes. It was a tidy little spread. Big red barn, cross-buck fencing, white clapboard house. The ranch had good water access, lots of pasture ground, workable leases and turned a marginal profit which in these times was about as good as it got. Most men would consider themselves lucky. And yet, nothing about the stipulations of Vi's will settled well.

"Doesn't matter how you feel about it," Nat Henderson, Vi's lawyer, had told him when he'd called yesterday after he'd received the letter, but before he'd left to attend Vi's funeral. "The document's legal and binding. You're the executor. It's your job to see to it the terms are carried out."

Executor. If Henderson had told him he'd won the lottery, he couldn't have shocked him more. And no, it didn't feel right.

Mouth set in a grim line, Trav continued on down the rise and into the lane. Bed sheets flapped in a stout July wind funneling down through the valley. Sooner snoozed in the grass beside the clothes basket, head down, long muzzle tucked between her paws.

It wasn't the dog or the postcard scene or even the long line of wash snapping in the wind, however, that captured Travis's attention and held it. It was the sight of Vi Hobson's prodigal stepdaughter. It was the punch of arousal—raw, sexual and as real as it got—that hit him in his gut and had him reining the gelding in. Had him drawing a deep, bothered breath.

He'd walked away from her yesterday denying to the nth degree that he had experienced any kind of physical reaction when he'd finally sought her out and found her there, worrying over Sooner. All night long, he'd dodged it, and when he couldn't duck it any longer, he'd argued that it was the shock of finally meeting her, the residual grief, the tension only a funeral could bring.

But one look at her this morning and he accepted defeat. He'd been blowing smoke. He'd been lying through his teeth. The woman made him hot. And he didn't like it.

He sat where he was, shifted in the saddle and watched her. She stood in the yard with her back to him. She was dressed in short, frayed cutoffs and a slim-fitting white knit tank top. Her bare arms were raised to the clothesline as she pinned a sheet to a length of cotton rope stretched between the house and detached garage.

Yesterday, he'd been ready for her, flanked by first the church crowd then a houseful of people as a buffer. He'd thought he'd been ready today.

Caught unprepared by the sight she made, home-spun and settled, female and fragile, he was suddenly defenseless against his reactions. Caught unprepared, his preconditioned hostility toward folks in general and women in particular didn't stand a chance. The only thing that did was appreciation. Purely male. Wholly sexual.

Silhouetted against the foothills and quaking aspen, she made an incredibly enticing, even erotic, picture. Her legs were bare, coltishly long, and exceptionally fine. The cheeks packed into those worn shorts were tight and tidy handfuls. From the back, her torso was slim, her waist high. As she tipped her head back and stretched to reach the line, her deep sable hair fell midway down her back. The wind caught it, lifted, swirled it around her head. With an absent gesture, she tossed her head so the heavy weight of it tumbled back behind her shoulder again.

And he plunged deeper into lust.

Pure. Spontaneous. Unqualified.

The instant reaction, gut-deep and intense, broadsided him. It came from as far out in left field as the cheap seats. And it was as wrong as a left turn on red.

"Whoa." The gelding stopped at his softly uttered command. He sucked in a deep breath, let it out, then felt his entire body stiffen when she bent over and dragged another sheet out of the basket. His pulse spiked then pooled in a rush to his groin.

"That does it." He had to get out of here. Needed a little distance to figure out what the hell was going on. He was thirty-eight, not sixteen. He was ruled by the head on his shoulders, not the one in his pants, and at the moment, he wasn't too pleased by the cues he was getting from either one.

He laid the reins over Max's neck with a prompt to turn and head back home, but just a little too late. Boomer wound into a yappy and frenzied schnauzer tirade. Sooner sprang to all fours, ears pricked forward, ready to defend. And Susannah spun around like she'd been shot, a pale green sheet clutched to her breasts.

Her blue eyes were wide and startled. And when her gaze lifted from the noisy schnauzer and she spotted him, it was apparent he'd missed his chance to escape. It was also apparent he'd scared her half to death.

The little collie walked slowly out to meet Boomer, who was now happily prancing and proud of the ruckus he'd raised. And while the dogs exchanged requisite sniffs, Travis sat where he was in the saddle, wishing the hell he'd resolved this issue with a phone call.

"Good morning," she said, making a shade with her hand as she squinted into the sun. She folded the sheet over her forearm and still holding it in front of her, walked toward him. "You startled me. At least your dog did."

Boomer, having already lost interest in the pregnant Sooner, trotted over beside her. With a typical lack of manners, he stood on his hind legs and stretched his front paws onto her thigh, begging for attention.

With a laugh that seemed more forced than spontaneous, she squatted down to pet him. "Aren't you a cutie." She glanced up, the smile tilting her lips not quite reaching her eyes. "Let me guess. He's a working dog, right?"

Travis pushed out a grunt, wondering why she was trying so hard to appear casual, hoping to hell he was pulling off the same thing. "About the only thing he works is me."

"I'll bet you know how to work him real good, too, don't you?" As she reached to scratch the little dog's ears, a gold chain swung away from the nest it had made between her full breasts. He recognized both the chain and the set of rings hanging from it as the ones Vi had always worn.

"What's his name?"

"The same as his MO. Boomer."

She laughed again. Again, it sounded forced, like she was trying too hard. "So you're a wild man, huh?" she murmured while Boomer ate up the attention with a spoon. "I had a friend who had a mini. Mouthiest little dog I've ever met. He thought he was as big as a Mack truck. Wouldn't back down from anything."

In spite of his determination to remain unaffected by the way she looked, by the edge in her voice, Trav had to bite back a smile at her accurate summation of the breed. "Yeah, well, you meet one, you've pretty much met 'em all."

Fighting the urge to follow the glint of gold disappearing beneath her top, he swung a leg over the saddle and dismounted. He ground-reined Max and nodded toward Sooner. "Had any luck?"

A small frown furrowed her brows. "I got a little milk down her last night, but she turned up her nose at her breakfast again this morning."

He turned his back to her, took his time digging into his saddlebag for the two tubes of paste supplement he'd brought with him. When he turned back to face her, he was in control again. He planned to keep it that way. "The fact that she took the milk's a good sign. Let's try some of this. Come here, little girl. Come on, Sooner."

Hunkered down and balancing on his boot tips,

Trav coaxed the dog to his side. "Each tube contains about five feedings for a dog her size and weight. Give her a couple a day. Just open her mouth, like this—there's a good girl—and place the tip as far back as you can and squeeze.

"There, that wasn't so bad now was it?" he praised the collie as he massaged her throat to encourage swallowing. "Got to take care of those babies. Got to take care of you."

When he rose, the smile tilting Susannah's lips was relaxed, genuine.

"What?"

She shrugged, clutched the sheet closer against herself. "You're very good with her. Very gentle. Kind."

"Yeah, well, I'm a sucker for a damsel in distress."

The moment the words were out, he wanted to take them back. He wasn't gentle. He wasn't kind. He'd played the roll of sucker once and he didn't want anyone mistaking him for someone who was willing to play it again.

"Let me go check on the barn stock and then if you have a minute, we can have that talk."

Her frown appeared to be in reaction to his scowl. "Fine. Come on up to the house when you're finished."

Without another word, he turned. Jaw set, he snagged Max's reins and headed for the barn. He didn't want to watch her walk on those long, slim legs to the house. Didn't want to witness the sweet sway of her hips, see the way her hair tumbled down her back like dark satin ribbons and curled loosely at the ends. Didn't want to think about that warm, dark place where gold nestled against smooth, pale flesh.

It was a hard kick in the pants to realize he didn't have to actually see her to imagine every little move and every little step she made. Even harder was the realization he wasn't nearly as bothered by the prospect of delivering his news as he was by his physical reaction to a woman he couldn't seem to stop thinking about dragging off to the nearest bed.

Four

Susannah had given up coffee for the baby's sake when she'd found out she was pregnant, but she took a chance on Travis Dean wanting some. The scent of it, fresh-brewed and strong, along with the scent of warm caramel rolls—compliments of Rachael Scott—filled the house as she set plates and butter and anything else she could think of that he might want on the kitchen table. She glanced out the window over the sink just in time to see him latch the barn door behind him and head out in long, purposeful strides toward the house.

Leaning a hip against the counter, she crossed her arms beneath her breasts and looked her fill. Everything about the man was big. Big steps, big shoulders, big presence. Big scowl. Yeah, the scowl was hard to miss, but on some level, she'd noticed those other things about him yesterday, too, even though most of the day had gone by in a blur.

He'd filled up his fair share of the pew at the church services and stood a head above most of the men at the graveside. When he'd found her sitting on the bottom porch step worrying over Sooner, he'd towered over her. But those assessments had been more peripheral impressions than studied observations. She took advantage of the opportunity to refine her assessment now—and to take her mind off the note she'd found in the storm cellar last night. She needed some distance from Vi's message and all of its disturbing implications.

He wasn't a young man. Late thirties, she decided. She wondered, again, if he was married. He was attractive, more than attractive, and it both surprised and bothered her that in spite of everything that had happened, she felt an unwarranted and unwise stirring of physical attraction toward him. He made quite a sight, did Mr. Dean, eating up the ground in long strides as he walked, head down, toward the house. He also did more than justice to a suit and tie, as well as the tight jeans straining over the thighs straddling the big sorrel he'd ridden into the yard.

But she wasn't going to ride that sunset path again. Whether rodeo riders or the real thing like Travis Dean, cowboys were her Achilles' heel. Loneliness and more uncertainty than she was willing to admit were neither just cause nor excuses to fall for another sexy package. She'd learned her lessons the hard way, but she'd learned them well. Physical attraction did not equate to love or commitment.

Besides, she wasn't even sure he liked her. He might be physically attracted to her, though. She'd noticed the way he'd looked at her. There'd been appreciation in his eyes. Reluctant, but it had been there.

He drew closer to the house, and the details she'd avoided noticing became glaringly obvious now. The hair beneath his brown Stetson was coarse and thick. It was neither blond nor brown, more the color of polished oak or of her father's buckskin stallion. The eyes the brim of his hat shadowed were a pale, cool blue, except when he addressed Sooner. They warmed then, gentled, and she suspected he'd be surprised to know they revealed a glimpse of a kind man since he seemed to have a need to guard that particular trait behind cold eyes and impassive glares.

"He thinks you're pretty special, doesn't he, girl?" she murmured to the collie who lay on the rug by the back door. "So we know he's not all growl and snarl."

He didn't have what she'd call a pretty face, not like Jason's had been pretty. Travis Dean's face, while pleasing, was too lived-in, too hard to be categorized as handsome. Hard. That was the word. His face was hard, but not in a used-up way. It seemed to be attitude more than genetics giving the impression of impenetrable, steely resolve, and she couldn't help but wonder what had made him feel the need to show it to her.

His chin was strong, his jaw wide in comparison to his nose which was straight and narrow. His mouth, when it wasn't compressed in a tight, grim line, was almost poetic, possibly even sensual. She wondered what he looked like when he smiled.

Shivering, she turned away from the window. Unaware, her fingers rose to worry the rings she still wore around her neck. Outside in the sun it was warm, but the kitchen held a leftover chill from the night. And like yesterday, still not knowing why, she suddenly felt cold in this man's presence. Grabbing an old flannel shirt from a hook by the back door, she shrugged into it. It hung on her like a tent, but she didn't care.

"Okay. Time to talk," she murmured under her breath as she headed for the back door when she heard his footsteps on the porch. "Come on in. Yeah, you, too, Boomer." She held the door open as the dog's toenails clicked across the white tile floor. "Something tells me he's made himself at home in this kitchen before."

"Yeah, well, Vi had a soft spot for him, though I never did understand why."

"It was probably the same soft spot he tapped in you. Some things just can't be explained. Go ahead. Sit down. I'm guessing you take your coffee black?"

He nodded, doffed his hat and pulled out a chair. She had to smile, just a little, as he sat and hooked his hat over one of the four ladder-back chairs flanking the table. He forked his fingers through his hair to comb out the ridge his hat had left. Then he stilled, looking like a big brooding bear chewing on what he'd come here to say to her.

"The rolls are warm," she said, pushing the plate toward him. "Go ahead. Help yourself."

When he mumbled, "Just coffee's fine, thanks," she knew he'd come to lecture. She wasn't in the mood.

She poured him a mug then joined him, folding her hands together on the top of the round oak table that had sat in the kitchen for as long as she had memories. The feel of the solid, familiar wood beneath her hands bolstered her confidence, as did the memories of all the meals she'd eaten here with her mom and dad, and the ones, later, with her dad and Vi.

"I want to thank you again for all you've done since Vi...since she died last week." The tears came fast and unexpected. She blinked them back, mortified.

"I'm sorry." She shook her head, embarrassed, and pressed her palms to her cheeks. "I thought I had that under control."

The chair creaked as he shifted his weight. "I imagine you're still working through it. It's been a lot to digest."

"Yeah, it has."

She was still struggling to get past the unexpected crush of pain when his next words brought her head up.

"Where did they find you?"

She didn't understand. "Find me?"

"To tell you about Vi." The cool blue of his eyes searched hers from beneath pinched brows. "Last I knew you'd been out of touch for several years. No one knew where you were. I know Vi didn't have an address. Del had been trying to find you to tell you what happened."

"Sheriff Brooks didn't *find* me." She shook her head, suddenly awash with guilt. "I was already on my way home."

At his stunned look she nodded. "Yeah. Good timing, huh?" She looked past him, out the kitchen window where snow-white clouds drifted against the blue Colorado sky. "Four years. It had taken me four years to swallow my pride, make the decision to come home and ask Vi to forgive me. Four years—and I was two days too late."

"You mean, you came back not knowing what had happened?"

"Exactly. I got home late on the night of the thirtieth. I was excited and happy and worried all at the same time as I pulled into the drive. There was so much I wanted to tell her." She stopped, swallowed. "So much she deserved to hear from me."

She blinked back another resurgence of tears, drew

a bracing breath. "She'd already been gone for three days."

He swore softly. "So you sat out here waiting alone...for how long?"

"Oh, not long. I called Clarence Peters, our old foreman, that same night. I thought maybe he could tell me where she was. I knew she couldn't be far. I mean, it was obvious she'd recently been in the house. Poor Clarence. He and Martha came over right away. It was hard for him to be the one to have to break the news."

"And it's been hard for you."

The gentleness in his tone surprised her. She didn't think he'd intended to offer compassion, but it was there, in the gaze she met and held. "You said you and Vi were friends. I imagine she told you the way things were when I left."

When he shifted in his chair, she figured she'd pinned down the reason for some of his discomfort around her. She decided to make it easy on him. "For what it's worth, I'm not very proud of the way I treated her. I know she didn't deserve it.

"Did you know her well?" she asked after the silence filled up with her regrets and became so heavy she couldn't bear it.

He nodded. "We worked our spreads together."

"Did she...ever talk about me?"

His gaze flicked to her hand, where she worried the rings, then to the mug of coffee he had yet to touch. "Yeah. She talked about you."

Until she'd asked and he'd answered, she hadn't realized how much she'd needed to know. "I hurt her badly, didn't I?"

He raised his gaze to hers, let out a breath and went

back to studying the mug. He smoothed his thumb absently over the handle. "I think she hurt more for you than she did for herself."

She tilted her head, studied his face. "And you don't figure I deserved her sympathy." It wasn't a question and she didn't expect an answer. She already had one. "Well, that makes two of us."

Restless suddenly, she rose and walked to the sink where she could look out the window to the hills in which she'd spent hours as a child riding her old pony, Spook. "Did you ever get do-overs when you were a little kid?" She didn't get a response, didn't expect one. "When I messed up, did something wrong and wanted another shot at it, I'd just say 'do-over' and I got another crack at it. You don't know how many times since I left here that I've wished I could have had a do-over where Vi was concerned."

Wrapping the loose shirt around herself to ward off another chill, she turned back to face the unreadable eyes of the man who seemed to fill up the kitchen with his brooding presence. When she spoke, it was more to herself than to him. "I can justify why I left a hundred different ways. I was young. I was foolish. I was angry and scared. I'd just lost my dad. Before that, I'd lost my mom. I adored her. And a year later, when Dad married Vi, I resented it when she tried to take her place…and then I hated myself and felt like I was betraying my mom when I felt that same kind of love for Vi."

She looked from him to Sooner, who slept on the rug at her feet. Tears of regret blurred her vision. "She tried so hard. And I gave her so much grief. Then when Dad died," she stopped, gathered herself. "I lost it. When I look back now, I think running was my way of making sure I didn't lose Vi, too. And God forbid I let her know losing her would hurt. So I left first. That way she couldn't very well leave me, could she?''

She forced a tight smile. ''Well, *that* didn't work, did it?'' Another pause. Another self-censuring smile. ''Man. Wouldn't a shrink have a field day with me and my abandonment issues?''

When he actually squirmed in his chair, she almost laughed, because, really, at this point there was nothing else she could do. ''Sorry, again. I hadn't planned to stage a little meltdown this morning, at least not in front of anyone.''

He leaned forward, wrapped both of his big hands around the coffee mug. ''Must have been something you needed to get off your chest.''

She had a lot of things she wanted to get off her chest. The message she'd found in the storm cellar was one of them. She almost told him then about the note, about her suspicions Vi had been killed. There was something about him—a steadiness that told her he was someone she could count on. And yet, something held her back.

Still, it was compelling to tell him, this man she sensed she could trust, but really didn't know. In the end, it was the deciding factor. She didn't know him, didn't have enough information to know if she *could* trust him. Or if she even needed to. Maybe a nice padded room with bars on the windows wasn't so far off her flight path after all.

''Yeah, well…moving right along,'' she said. ''You came over here for a reason and I'm sure you've got better things to do than play therapist.''

* * *

She was right about that, Trav thought as she sat in expectant silence. He did have a reason for being here—although there were a million things he'd rather do than initiate this conversation.

He'd given it a lot of thought, enough that he'd decided it might be wiser to simply find out what her plans were before he broke the news about the will. Maybe he was sweating this for nothing. Maybe she had a realistic handle on what was best for her, and all this drama over the Rocking H would be moot.

"I was hoping we could talk about the ranch," he began carefully. "It's not a particularly big operation, but that doesn't negate the volume of work it takes to keep things running."

"Oh. Of course," she said as if it finally dawned on her why he was here. That guilt was the response he was after. "You can't continue doing the work at both your spread and this one. And of course, I'll…well, I'll figure out a way to compensate you for what you've done so far."

He held up a hand. "Whoa. That's not what I meant. I don't expect compensation. I'd be offended if you offered. I told you. Vi and I were friends."

"Just the same, you can't continue—"

He cut her off again with a shake of his head. "I can. And I will. Until you decide what you're going to do, I can cover what needs to be done here and at my place."

"Until I decide what I'm going to do?"

She looked so utterly confused, he decided maybe he might be treading on ground she hadn't even approached, let alone walked. Before he could decide how to broach it, she did it for him.

"You're right, of course. I do need to make some

decisions. I need to figure out the best way to—'' She broke off, frowned. ''Well, the best way to do a lot of things. It's been awhile. I'll have a lot to relearn, I'm afraid. And I'll need to hire some fulltime help.''

''You don't need to hire anyone. I can fill in long enough for you to get things in order and get the place on the market.''

He hadn't meant to have it slip out that way. And when she looked at him like he'd suggested she set the house on fire, he realized what a huge mistake he'd made.

''You think I want to sell the ranch?''

''I think,'' he said carefully, wishing that was exactly what she wanted to do, ''you probably haven't thought past today.''

She walked back to the table, sat down with a weary breath. ''If only. But the truth is, I haven't done anything *but* think. About today. About yesterday. About a lot of yesterdays.'' Her voice was so soft, he had to strain to hear her. ''And I have thought about tomorrow.''

When those blue eyes met his, he felt an unexpected punch of both empathy and of arousal that had no place in this conversation, no place in any of his reactions to her.

''I've come home, Mr. Dean. Too late to make things right with Vi, but I'm finally home. It took me too long to get back here. I don't plan to leave again any time soon.''

He compressed his lips, made himself concentrate on what she'd said, instead of on the look of her or his unexpected respect for her, or his unwarranted physical responses. What she'd said was exactly what he'd been afraid of hearing.

"This life isn't easy." He'd been shooting for reason, but even to his ears he sounded condescending. It didn't stop him from trying again. "I don't think you're considering that. It was difficult for Vi and she was seasoned and tough with ten years of experience and know-how to back her up. You've been away for a long time. Maybe too long to make this kind of rash decision without considering the consequences."

She smiled then, a small, sad, weary little smile. It should have made her look younger. Instead, it added more age to the eyes that already looked far too old for someone so young. "I've got a history of rash decisions to draw from. Believe me, coming home and planning to stay aren't among them."

"Then you're not facing facts," he said more gruffly than he'd intended. "You don't have a clue what you'd be letting yourself in for."

"You forget I grew up here."

"You forget you left and you were never alone before."

If possible, her face turned a whiter shade of pale. "I've never forgotten. Not for a minute. It was the biggest mistake of my life."

He was surprised by her quick recovery and by the flame of anger flaring in her blue eyes. If he hadn't been so uneasy about this whole damn mess, he would have appreciated that spark of life, maybe even celebrated it.

But this was no time for celebration. It sounded like she'd dug her heels in good and deep. And it was going to make it just that much harder to break the news about the will.

Susannah had run the gamut of emotions from appreciation, to speculation to confusion over his insistence that he knew what was best for her. Right now, however, she was doing her darnedest to hold her temper. Where did he get off, trying to tell her what to do? What business was it of his anyway?

For the sake of decorum, she tried to see things from his perspective. He was Vi's friend. She certainly owed him for everything he'd done. Maybe he felt he had some ownership here. Well, he didn't and she'd like to tell him as much flat out. But she was going to be living next to this man. She couldn't afford to alienate him. So she tried, for both of their sakes, to keep it light.

"Okay. If I understand correctly, you feel the best thing all around would be for me to sell out and go back to whatever life I was living before I had the nerve to show my face around these parts again," she finished in her best, get-out-of-Dodge gunslinger voice.

He wasn't amused. Well, fine. That made two of them. She tilted her head, looked him in the eye. "For what you've done for Vi, for what you've done for me, I owe it to you to listen, so finish saying your piece and I'll finish mine."

He looked at her like he was trying to figure out if she was in her right mind, zoned out on drugs or just plain stupid. Since he was going to draw his own conclusions about her no matter what she said, she didn't bother to tell him it was none of the above.

"Look," he began again, "I know this has been hard on you, but you need to be thinking with a clear head here, not reacting to what you wish could have been different and how you wish things could be."

"Since you have apparently decided that I'm not

thinking clearly, help me out here. What would a clearheaded person think?''

"That running this operation is a lot to chew off.''

"A lot to chew off for a woman? Tell me, does your wife put up with that attitude or does she simply overlook it?''

If possible, his eyes grew even harder. "I don't have a wife.''

"I think I'm beginning to see why.'' She smiled to take the bite out of her comment. He did not smile back.

"I'm not into gender bashing. I'm stating facts.''

"Which, to your way of thinking, are?''

He glared at her. "Vi spent six years working by Dale's side and four on her own, learning the business, toughening up, studying market trends and pulling calves and doctoring stock. She was a remarkable person. If any woman could handle the workings of a Colorado cattle ranch and survive the rigors of mountain winters, she was the one.''

"And I'm not her.''

He regarded her with a patience he clearly had to dig deep to find. "And *she* couldn't do it, either. The last four years were hard on her. She carried on for Dale. She carried on for you. But she was tired, Susannah. She was ready to throw in the towel.''

Guilt piled on top of guilt. She should have been here to help her. "She had a right to be tired. She wasn't a young woman.''

"And you are, but youth is no substitute for brawn. At least not in a woman. That's a law of nature, not an opinion.''

Oh, he had opinions, she was sure of it. She was also pretty sure she didn't want to hear them, not as they pertained to her. "You don't need to lecture me about the workings of a cattle ranch. I've been gone, yes, but I grew up here. I worked the ranch, too. I know what I'm up against. I know I need help. I'm prepared to hire someone."

"I helped," he said flatly. "It was still too much for her."

"And you clearly don't want to help me. Is that what all this is about, because—"

"I didn't say that."

"You didn't have to. And that's fine. You've done more than enough. I'll talk to Clarence—"

He cut her off with a shake of his head. "Clarence would do anything for you, but he's not fit to sit a saddle anymore, whether he'll admit it or not. His hips are arthritic, his blood pressure's sky high and he's feeling his age in a way that makes him want to believe he's still got what it takes to wrangle cattle."

God, he must really dislike her. "I would not take advantage of Clarence. And I didn't intend to ask him to wrangle cattle."

"So *you* were going to do that part?"

She propped her elbows on the table, rubbed her temples with her fingertips and wished she'd never let the conversation get this far. She didn't have to justify her decisions to him and yet she felt just defensive enough that she wanted to let him know she wasn't an airhead without any mind for business. "At some point, yeah. In the meantime, Rachael's boys—"

"Oh, wait. Whoa." He shook his head, let out an incredulous snort. "Clay and Jed Scott?"

"Yes. Clay and Jed Scott," she said, bristling at his condescending tone.

"Clay is just out of high school and Jed can't be more than seventeen."

"They're both looking for work."

"No. *Rachael* is looking for work *for* them. Trust me on this. You do *not* want the Scott boys at the Rocking H."

"Then I'll put an ad in the paper."

"And handle things *how* until someone whom you won't know, can't trust and will probably be gone when you advance him his first paycheck answers it?"

The chair scraped like chalk on a blackboard when she stood, suddenly out of patience, out of tolerance and out of time for Travis Dean. She may have been used to dealing with cow-*boys,* not men, and though Travis Dean definitely fell into the latter category, he was the same gender. She'd had a bellyful of the opposite sex, thank you very much. And she'd just reached her limit with this man in particular.

"I don't know what your angle on this is. Whether you want to buy the Rocking H for yourself, or if you've got a buddy with some money to burn who wants to play rancher. But—"

"Now wait just a damn minute."

"No. You wait." Travis Dean didn't scare her, not even when he stood, uncoiling all six-plus feet and towering over her with his size. "I'm not about to kowtow or knuckle under to yet one more male who postures and spouts about logic and my best interests. Not when experience has taught me the only real interest a man has ever had in me has been in how fast he could get me on my back and how long he could keep me there before I started making noises about forever."

She was shaking with fury now—at the cowboys who had left her, at Jason Murphy for not owning up, at Travis Dean for lording over her like he possessed some omnipotent power and all the answers.

"I'm don't know who or what you think you're dealing with here, but I'm not stupid. I know what I'm getting into.

"Have I made poor choices? Too many to count." She stopped, settled herself, trying not to think about her poor choices when it came to the men who had drifted in and out of her life and left her, always, with nothing. "But staying on at the Rocking H isn't one of them.

"Look," she continued before he could formulate a comment, "I'm not sure why you think you have a say or even a need to tell me what's best for me, but whether you like it or not, I'm not going anywhere. You don't want to help? Okay. Don't help. I don't expect you to and you certainly aren't under any obligation. But I *do* have obligations and I have a debt to pay.

"I owe Vi," she said and fought to keep guilt from slowing her momentum. "Is it too little, too late? Absolutely. For that I'll always be sorry. But I also owe it to myself. And I owe it to my baby."

Even through her anger—at herself over the mistakes she'd made, at life for taking this grim turn of events, and at him for judging her without knowing her—she was aware of the color draining from his face, of the sudden rigidity of his big body.

"Baby?" He looked from her face to her hands, narrowed his eyes as he focused on her waist that was lost in the folds of the flannel shirt. "You're pregnant?" The question came out on a hoarse whisper

of disbelief, as if she'd just told him the world was going to come to its long overdue end in about thirty more seconds. He was more than surprised by her statement. He was discouraged. And she'd be damned if she could figure out why.

"Yes." She watched him warily as outside she heard the sound of tires crunching on gravel. "I thought it was pretty obvious."

"Nothing," he muttered as he strode past her toward the door, "is ever obvious."

Five

"Pregnant," Trav grumbled under his breath as he stormed out of the kitchen and onto the back porch. He stopped on the bottom step, hooked his hands on his hips and stared into space. "Didn't it just figure? Didn't it just goddamn figure?"

So what did he expect? Why was he even surprised? She'd run at eighteen. God knew what she'd done, where she'd been, whom she'd run with. And now she was pregnant. That was why she'd come back.

Her return had nothing to do with reconciliation with Vi. She was in trouble. She needed help. Had the guy run out on her, he wondered. What had she said? Something about the only interest a man had ever had in her was how fast he could get her on her back and how long he could keep her there.

Is that what had happened? Had she been fed a line of lies, too? Is that why she was alone and pregnant?

He wondered why the hell he was surprised or even angry about it. Or why he even cared.

He dragged a hand over his face. Exclusive of the unwanted physical attraction he felt for her, she'd gotten to him with those big blue eyes and all her talk about remorse and mistakes. Well, he'd heard that kind of song and dance before and had even believed it—and it had cost him everything. His pride, his business, his marriage. Six long damn months of his life. He knew better than to fall for it. And yet, he had.

The slam of a car door had him jerking his head toward the driveway. He hadn't noticed Del's cruiser pull up. Boomer heard the door slam, and inside the house the little dog launched into a barrage of ear-piercing barks. Sooner even managed a couple of watchdog-worthy woofs as Del leaned back in through the open driver's side window and picked up something from the seat.

About the same time, the screen door creaked open and the schnauzer shot down the steps like a fuzzy rocket, ready to lay into the sheriff like Del didn't stand five-ten and weigh in at around two-fifty.

"Hey, Trav, how's it going? Oh, be quiet, you little yapper," Del sputtered around a grin as he tossed Boomer a doggy treat from the stash he always carried with him. He angled Trav a pitying look. "Got to be hard on a man's ego keeping company with a worthless excuse of a dog like that one. You're a better man than me, boyo."

"Yeah, well, we all have our crosses to bear." Trav managed a half-hearted grin, well aware that Del had never met a dog he didn't like or passed on an opportunity to give him a good-natured ribbing.

Del was a far cry from the slim little kid with a fishing pole perpetually glued to his hand when they'd met as boys all those years ago. He sported a barrel belly now, along with a quick smile that left deep creases around his gray eyes.

"Now *there's* a dog." Del bent over with a grunt to offer Sooner a treat. "How about you, little missy? You want one, too?

"Still mourning, huh?" he asked with a frown when Sooner sniffed, but refused his handout. She walked back to the porch and sat down by Susannah who had come out to see what had gotten Boomer so excited.

"Hello there, Susannah. How you doin' today?"

From the corner of his eye, Trav saw the terse smile she gave the sheriff. "I'm doing fine, Sheriff. Thanks."

Involuntarily, Trav's gaze strayed to her waistline and the small, hard mound of her abdomen. How had he missed it? Same way he'd missed a lot of other things in his life, he thought grimly. He hadn't been paying attention—at least not to the things that had counted. Yesterday, he'd seen a slim, grieving woman lost in a black sack of a dress. Today, he'd seen a long length of leg and a tidy behind. And in her kitchen, he'd seen a flannel shirt that hung past the hem of her shorts and covered what was now a very obvious rounding of her belly.

Nope. He hadn't been paying attention. Story of his life. Well, he'd picked a hell of a time to start paying attention now. He didn't need this; he didn't need any of it.

"I've got some news for you, Susannah," Del said soberly. Walking up to the porch, he propped his foot on the bottom step. "It's about what happened to Vi."

Whether he needed it or not, Trav was too aware when Susannah crossed her arms beneath her breasts and braced herself. Fighting an unexpected urge to wrap an arm around her shoulder to help cushion the blow, he clenched his jaw and looked away.

"Close as we can figure, the other person must

have come up over the rise behind her. As best as we can piece it together, Vi spotted the car in her rear-view mirror and was afraid she was going to get rear-ended so she hit the gas.

"The county had just graded the road. You know how that is—makes it slick as ball bearings for a few days. Anyway," he continued, compelled to fill the silence when Susannah stood statue still, "they both lost control and went over the side.

"It's officially going down as an accident," he added. "Just wanted to tell you in person, instead of over the phone."

"What about the other person?" she asked quietly.

Still angry over the news of her pregnancy, Trav told himself he was reading more into her question than was there. He sensed suspicion, which didn't make any sense.

"You still haven't found out anything about him or her?" she asked.

Del shook his head. "Not a darn thing. I'm sorry to paint such a grisly picture, but the body was burned pretty badly. It'll be a while before we get a sex established, much less an ID. We're running a statewide check on dental records right now. If that doesn't turn anything up, we'll go nationwide."

"You figure it was a tourist?" Trav asked, curious himself over the identity of the mysterious driver.

Again, Del shrugged. "Best guess, yeah. We've been trying to trace the car, but there weren't any license plates on it, and the registration or anything else of help burned to ash in the fire. It's going to be a while until we get anything solid."

"Are you sure it wasn't deliberate?"

Both men cut their gazes to Susannah.

"The wreck. Are you sure it wasn't deliberate?" she repeated, her face as pale as chalk, the anxiety in her voice as thick as the sudden tension filling the air.

"Deliberate?" Del's usually jovial expression turned grave. He looked from Susannah to Trav. Trav shrugged. He didn't know where this was coming from.

"Now, honey," Del said kindly, "what on earth possessed you to even ask such a question?"

She walked to the edge of the porch, wrapped her arm around a post as if she needed to steady herself. "I...well, you mentioned the license plates. How could there not be any plates on the car? Doesn't it seem strange?"

Del dismissed her concern with a shake of his head. "Could be lots of explanations for that. For instance, whoever it was could have just bought the car and had one of those temporary paper licenses stuck in the rear window."

"Susannah," Trav said, a sudden unease over her suggestion overshadowing his other feelings about her. "Is there something you know that we don't? I mean, hell. Deliberate? Vi? Who would want to hurt her?"

She wouldn't meet his eyes or Del's for that matter. "I don't know. I don't even know where that came from. It's just, well, Rachael Scott mentioned Vi had been gone on and off a lot lately. And that she'd been acting kind of strange—anxious, nervous. I'd chalked it up to Rachael being Rachael until, well..." She turned to Trav. "*Had* she been gone?"

He shrugged. "Some. She told me she had family back east and she'd decided it was time to reconnect with them. Asked me to watch Sooner and the spread while she went to visit.''

"I never heard her talk about any family." Her brows furrowed as if she were combing her memory for something she might have missed. "No," she decided finally. "As a matter of fact, I asked her about it once, about where she'd come from. She'd said she was born back east, that she had no brothers or sisters, and her mother and father died just before she moved to Colorado.''

"Well," Del put in calmly, "I agree, it does sound a bit out of sync, but lots of folks have secrets. Maybe a branch of the family they're ashamed of?" he suggested. "Could be she did have some folks—a brother or sister or something. You know, sometimes people get of an age when they start thinking of the choices they've made and maybe want to make some of those wrong choices right again.''

It was all Trav could do to keep from connecting with Susannah's gaze as Del more or less validated everything she'd said in her kitchen a little while ago about herself. People made mistakes. She'd made her share. Well, so had he, yet here he stood, more than ready to judge her.

"You're probably right," she said softly, but not sounding convinced. "I suppose I was just looking for something to help make sense of it. The idea that she simply drove off a road she knew like the back of her hand... Well, it's hard to swallow.''

Trav sensed there was something more, something she wasn't telling them, but he held his silence because he didn't want to get any deeper into any part of her life than he already was.

"It's only natural to try to come up with something

other than a twist of fate to explain away the loss of someone we care about," Del continued kindly. "You're not the first person to go looking for a better answer. Believe me, I've seen it a lot in my three terms as sheriff.

"Anyway, it'll get better. I know it sounds clichéd, but time does heal. You just hang in there, honey. In the meantime, I hate to bother you with this, but I need you to sign something for me. It's a release to the insurance company authorizing our office to give them a copy of our official report. They need it so they can release Vi's life insurance settlement. I'll just go get it from the car."

Trav felt a twinge of sympathy for her as even more color drained from her face. He couldn't help it. She looked lost and alone and suddenly overwhelmed with emotion as she turned and, without a word, walked back into the house, Sooner trailing her like a shadow.

Trav struggled with a compulsion to go after her, but made himself stand his ground as Del walked back to the porch with his clipboard.

Del glanced toward the kitchen door. "Hit her again, did it?"

He cleared his throat. "Apparently."

"I was afraid of that. This is another part of the job I could do without." Del paused, frowned. "Is she, ah... Well, folks were talking in town after seeing her at the funeral. Now that I've seen her, it appears they might be right. She really is pregnant, huh?"

Trav nodded, feeling like a fool for missing what

hadn't gotten past Del, or anyone else for that matter. "So it seems."

"No daddy in sight?"

"Doesn't appear to be."

Del stared at his clipboard, tapped it with his thumb. "Well, there's a wrinkle that'll add to her troubles."

Again, all Trav could do was nod.

"Suppose I could leave these with you?" Del pulled out the papers from the clipboard, folded them in half and extended them. "Just have her sign them and send them back when she's feeling up to it."

"I'll take care of it."

"It's a good thing, what you're doing here. Helping her out and all like you helped Vi."

Trav swallowed back a knee-jerk denial. There wasn't anything good about it. He'd helped Vi because he'd liked her. He'd helped Susannah because of Vi. And, until yesterday, because he'd thought it would be temporary. Susannah didn't know it yet, but Vi had set things up so *his* business at the Rocking H could be as permanent as he wanted it. It was Susannah's long-term involvement that was up for grabs.

"Has she said what she plans to do about the ranch?" Del asked, hiking up his pants, which seemed in a perpetual southward slide beneath the heavy girth of his belly.

"Says she plans to stay on," Trav said quietly.

Del pursed his lips, let out a low whistle. "Well now. That's gonna be a bit of a trick, her being alone and all. And with a baby no less. Suppose she's got a clue what she's in for?"

Travis pushed out a weary grunt. "Best guess? Not one."

"So you'll be helping her out, too, I reckon."

"At least until she decides that she's had enough," he said, not wanting to go into the will with Del. "I don't figure it'll be too long."

"Well, like I said, you're a better man than me, in more ways than one. I got to be goin'. Lester down at the hardware is madder than a hornet at the Scott boys and wants me to 'send 'em up the river til they rot,' I believe were his exact words."

Despite the somber mood, Travis had to grin. "What'd they do now?"

"Don't know yet if they did anything, but last night someone painted 'LESTER SUCKS'—" Del paused, peered around Travis toward the kitchen to see if Susannah was within earshot and decided not to take any chances. "Well, you can fill in the blank. Anyway, it's on the sidewalk in front of the store—in bright red oil-base paint no less—and like about everything else that happens around here, he's certain Clay and Jed are behind it."

"Not that they've ever been guilty of anything," Trav said dryly.

"Uh-huh. Anyway, I'm on my way over there to give 'em a little come-to-Jesus speech then listen to Rachael go on about why it is that every time something bad happens, her boys get blamed." He grunted. "Woman's got her head buried so deep in the sand she's gonna sprout ostrich feathers on her ass."

It felt good to chuckle.

"The things I do for my constituents," Del grumbled around a grin. "See you 'round, bud. Don't take any wooden nickels."

Trav waved as Del pulled out of the driveway. Then he just stood there, watching the cruiser's dust trail as it headed south toward the Scott place.

He stared toward the barn where, irony of ironies, Vi's mare was due to foal any day. He'd also spotted two calicos with fat bellies that could only mean the skittish tomcat that prowled the rafters had been a busy boy.

He looked over his shoulder toward the house, thought of Sooner and the woman inside.

This was the most pregnant damn place he'd ever seen.

He itched to get out of here. Go back to his own business and leave her well enough alone.

But he was going to have to go back in there.

He was going to have to tell her about the will. And then he was going to try to convince her that leaving was the only real option she had.

"Susannah?"

Susannah looked over her shoulder, surprised to hear his voice. She'd heard the sheriff's car pull out and figured Mr. Good Neighbor Dean would have retrieved his horse from the barn and been on his way over the ridge by now, too.

"I'm in the den," she said from the desk that held Vi's computer and possibly more secrets. She clutched the rings hanging on the chain around her neck. Their warmth and weight felt both comfortable and chilling and kept Vi's message close in her thoughts at all times.

The sheriff was convinced the car crash was an accident. She wasn't sure why she hadn't told him she had a compelling reason to suspect otherwise.

Possibly because Travis Dean was there and she didn't think it was any of his business. Or maybe because she simply didn't have it in her to deal with it right now.

"You all right?" she heard him ask from behind her.

She turned and saw him standing tall and broad-shouldered in the doorway. A scowl of concern dug deep creases between his brows. She couldn't figure him out. He was a complete enigma to her as he straddled the line between veiled hostility and sage advice on his take about what was best for her. Threaded through it all appeared to be genuine interest. And then there was the reaction to her pregnancy. He'd been angry. Casting moral judgment? Somehow it didn't feel like a good fit. Neither did the news of Vi's life insurance.

"I thought the funeral felt final," she said to herself as much as to him. "But life insurance..." She stared at the hands she'd clasped in her lap. "I hadn't even thought about it. Didn't know she had any.

"Well." She looked up, met his eyes. "It can't get much more final than that, can it?"

"She would have wanted you to take comfort in the notion that she provided for you."

She smiled, grateful. It was something she'd needed to hear right now.

"She's really gone, isn't she?" In spite of the ritual of the funeral and the grieving she'd done, it had taken the existence of the life insurance policy to make the finality of death sink in. "I'm never going to get to talk to her. I'm never going to get to tell her I'm sorry. She's never going to see my baby."

She didn't know how much time passed before she

heard the creak of an old floorboard beneath the faded carpet and looked up to find him standing directly in front of her.

"Is there anything I can do?"

Kind, she thought suddenly. Beneath all of his misplaced, but well-intentioned suggestions, behind his cold hard eyes, and all of his mixed signals, he was a kind man and he truly felt compelled to help. He just didn't know how. More importantly, he didn't want to, but couldn't seem to help himself.

Maybe it explained the difficulty he was having dealing with her. Well, that made two of them. She didn't have the strength to deal with him right now, either. She was suddenly very tired.

"No. Thanks for offering. I just need some time." *Alone* was implied, though not stated. She knew she was being rude, but she needed the space to think this all through.

"I'll be going, then. I'll be back tonight to check on your mare and on the pump south of the barn. I had to replace a valve yesterday and I want to make sure it's still working."

"Thanks. I appreciate it. I do. Appreciate it," she restated, needing him to know that in spite of her earlier anger, in spite of his, she was grateful for all the work he'd done to keep the Rocking H going.

He nodded, then, looking apologetic, extended the papers he'd all but crushed in his big hands. "Del left these. He asked that when you're up to it, you sign them and get them back to him. No hurry."

She took them from a hand that was not only big, but tanned and scarred. "Thanks. I'll take care of it."

His eyes were dark and solemn as he watched her, this man who didn't want to like her, didn't want to be here, but who just kept showing up to help her anyway.

She could tell he wanted to say something else. Just like she could tell when he decided that whatever it was, it could wait. Without another word, he turned and left her alone.

She set the insurance papers aside, added them to the mounting pile of mail on the desk. In the process, the fat manila envelope with the return address: Nathaniel Henderson, Attorney, fell to the floor. She bent to pick it up, debated for a moment and finally decided she couldn't avoid opening it any longer. She knew Vi's will was inside. What she didn't know was whether she was ready to face yet one more item of proof of the finality of her death.

The afternoon sun burned July hot on his back and shoulders as Trav bent over a flat tire on the hayrack. From the corner of his eye, he saw a trail of dust snake along the road as he fit a wrench around a lug nut. Grunting with the effort of loosening it, he reached for the can of WD-40 and sprayed the rusted fitting when it didn't budge. He was not a mechanic, at least he hadn't been when he'd taken on the ranch three summers ago.

He hadn't been a carpenter, either, but that had changed real fast, too. The thing about a working ranch was that it didn't work unless the machinery did, the gates opened and closed and barn doors held. It was rare if a week went by without something needing repair.

There was something else he hadn't been: a coward. That was what he felt like today, though, when he'd walked away from Susannah without letting her know how things stood with Vi's will. It wasn't the thought of the confrontation as much as it was his physical reaction to her that had him justifying putting it off.

He wiped a trickle of sweat away from his forehead with the back of his hand then squinted against the sun as an older model Blazer rolled into his lane. Tossing the wrench in his tool bucket, he snagged the shirt he'd discarded from the fence post where he'd hung it and shrugged into it. He didn't bother to button it. It was too hot. Besides, he wasn't expecting anyone. They could take him as he was.

Wiping his hands on a grease rag, he watched the vehicle, which was going way too fast, skid to a stop in front of the house. It wasn't until the driver's side door flew open that he recognized his visitor was Susannah.

His gut clenched at the sight of her. She looked like a warrior standing there, shoulders back, breasts arched forward, her cheeks as red as fire.

Well, well. Looked like he was going to get his chance to tell her about the will after all. Or judging by the look on her face, and the fist full of papers crushed in her hand, she was going to tell him a thing or two.

"Down here," he called, hooking a boot heel on the bottom rung of the wooden fence and folding his forearms over the top.

Then he waited as she marched across the drive, over the stretch of lawn circling it and butting up against the stockyard fence. Rather than walk the extra twenty yards to open a gate, she scaled the fence to get to him.

Pissed, he thought, watching her. Royally pissed.

Her hair flew wild about her face as the wind caught it, tugged it this way and that. Her cheeks were bright red splashes of color beneath eyes that were narrowed and latched on him like laser beams. It wasn't just the fire in her eyes that made him feel like he was burning.

He set his jaw, arranged his face to hide any emotion that might give him away and waited. She had a thing or two to tell him, all right. All he had to do was deal with the fallout and keep his libido under wraps.

The letter and the will Susannah clutched in her hand fueled a rage that had red spots swimming in front of her eyes, fed a fear that made her knees wobble.

She vibrated with rage as she squared off directly in front of him. "You knew about this."

With maddening indifference, he glanced at the bulging envelope she'd found with a bundle of mail that had sat, unopened, on the desk in the den beside the computer until an hour ago. She had no doubt the letter and the copy of the will stuffed inside it were identical to the ones he had also received.

"Yeah," he said, without apology and without excuses. "I knew. I got my letter yesterday, just before I left for the funeral."

"And you didn't think it was important enough to bring up?"

"Yesterday? No. You had enough to deal with. It was my intention to talk to you when I came over this morning."

"But somehow it what—slipped your mind?"

The look he gave her, as his blue eyes shifted from

her face to the packet of papers, was unreadable. "Let's go up to the house and talk about this."

"I don't want to go up to the house. I want some answers. Now."

She felt like she was crawling out of her skin. Even the depth and the breadth of the Colorado sky seemed too small to contain her anger and betrayal. It had swept over her like a prairie fire, sped up her heart rate and flushed her face with heat when she'd read the letter and the stipulations of the will.

She hadn't wanted to believe what she was reading. She'd *wanted* to believe she'd been right about him. That Travis Dean was a nice guy, well-intentioned, if a little off base. Wrong. She'd been so wrong. It was all here in this letter. Cut and dried.

Travis Dean was not a nice man. What he was, was an unscrupulous opportunist. Somehow, he'd managed to make himself executor of Vi's will. He was also a beneficiary—subject to certain conditions. If Susannah was not located within two years of Vi's death, the Rocking H went to Travis, free and clear. If she was located within the two-year period, but didn't want to stay, Travis had first option to buy at thirty percent below market value with the proceeds going to Susannah. If she decided to stay, however, she and Travis owned the Rocking H jointly. Susannah retained full rights to the house and half the land and would be entitled to half the annual profits. If Travis opted to sell his half, however, rather than partner up with her, Susannah could buy him out or sell her half as well and the proceeds would be split fifty-fifty.

She'd reread every stipulation twice to make sure she understood. Unfortunately, she understood all too well. And now she was looking into the eyes of the man who had maneuvered himself into a position of controlling her future.

Her face burned with anger; her heart hammered with panic. The hand gripping the letter trembled with disbelief and a disappointment she had no right to feel, but felt anyway.

"Well," she said, swallowing back the bitter taste of defeat, "this certainly explains a lot of things, doesn't it? I mean, no wonder you felt you were in a position to advise me on what I should do. And no wonder you were in such a rush to convince me to sell. According to this, you make out like a bandit if I do. Of course, my bet is you're wishing I hadn't come back at all. Then in two years you'd really hit the gravy train."

He had nothing to say to that. He just gathered the scattering of tools spread out on the ground around the hay rake and tossed them one by one into a bucket.

"Say something, damn you!" Never in her life had she wanted to hit something like she wanted to hit that hard, granite jaw.

"Seems to me, you're the one who's got something to say."

She met his cold eyes with defiance and when he only stared back with the same intractable look on his face, her fury burst, wild and uncontrollable. "And you're the one with all the power, so what good would it do me?"

He turned his back on her and walked toward the gate.

"Don't you walk away from me," she demanded, storming after him.

He stopped. His shoulders rose and fell on a weary breath. "It's my turf. That makes it my choice. I'm going to the house. You can follow me and we can talk this out where it's cool, or you can stand here in the sun and bake. That's your choice. Of course, you can always run away again, like you ran before when things didn't go the way you wanted."

She felt her face flame.

"Come up to the house, Susannah," he said, then managed to grind out a weary, "Please. And just listen for a minute."

Six

Since it was apparent the only way she was going to get anything out of him was to follow him, Susannah finally submitted. Not that he seemed to care if she was behind him or not. Once he started walking he didn't bother to look back. He did stop and hold the door open for her, however, when she mounted the porch steps behind him and reluctantly walked inside.

It had been years since she'd been inside Charlie and Treva Dean's kitchen. Despite her anger, memories assailed her, of strong coffee brewing in the old-fashioned aluminum percolator that sat on the back burner of a huge white gas stove. Apple and raisin spice cake cooling on a baking rack on the scarred white countertop. The scent of Charlie's cherry-wood pipe tobacco mingling with the smoke of a wood fire glowing in the potbellied stove in the corner of the room.

The old house had absorbed those long-living and pleasant scents and welcomed her today like an old friend. A shiny stainless steel coffeemaker had replaced the percolator, but other than that, Treva's kitchen remained pretty much the same. A well-used Mission oak table and chairs were pushed up against the south wall. Instead of a fresh or dried floral arrangement like Treva had always centered on the honey-hued oak, a thin layer of dust was the table's only adornment, unless you counted the assortment of keys, a pocket knife and the stack of papers matching the ones she held in her hand.

"Sit," he said absently as he headed for the sink, pushed up his sleeves and turned on the faucet.

She sat, not wanting to watch him—tall and lean and capable standing at Treva's kitchen sink where he scrubbed his hands then lowered his head to splash water over his face and the back of his neck.

She didn't want to be aware of the way his working-man's jeans hugged his long legs and lean hips. And she didn't want to notice that his faded chambray shirt hung unbuttoned across his broad chest and rib cage. A chest that was sparsely dusted with pale gold hair. A rib cage that was lean and tanned and narrowed down to a flat abdomen.

She didn't want to be aware of any of it. But she was. Even through her anger—maybe because of it and the sensory overload that came with it—she was aware of too much masculinity, too much sex appeal. And pregnant or not, she was way too aware of her own physical reaction.

His body didn't have the same toned, tight definition of Jason's, which was all sinewy strength and six-pack abs. But Jason was twenty-three. A boy. Travis Dean was a man. The years showed—in the creases around his eyes, in the body that was whipcord lean, in the hands that he dried with a towel and were scarred from the rigors of life on a ranch.

Without a word, he reached into the refrigerator and pulled out a water jug. He poured two glasses, set one in front of her and downed the other in long, thirsty gulps. Then he poured another. After wiping the towel over his face and neck, he tossed it toward the sink. Glass in hand, he sat down across from her at the table.

He let out a deep breath and leaned forward, his elbows propped on the table, his hands clasped in front of him. It was his hands he focused on while he seemed to consider what he was going to say. It was the water droplets clinging to his hair and the heavy fringe of his lashes that held her captive as he notched his chin toward his copy of the will laying open on the table.

"I did not ask for this."

His words were a stark, harsh reminder of why she was here and of what he'd managed to accomplish. She jerked her gaze away from his hands, met his hard stare with one of her own. "Of course you didn't."

She knew her sarcasm registered, but he chose to ignore it. "And just so you know, I've already checked with Henderson. The terms of the will are binding. According to him, Vi was determined it was what she wanted to do."

"With a little encouragement from you?"

He lifted his head, met her eyes. "You're going to believe what you want, but I'm going to tell it like it is. I didn't know about this and I don't want any part of it. The fact remains, I'm as stuck with it as you are."

"You're right. I don't believe it."

He pushed out a weary snort, forked his fingers through his hair. "If I were in your shoes I wouldn't believe it, either."

Planting his forearms back on the table, he stared at his hands again, tapped his thumbs together as if searching for what he wanted to say. "Look," he said finally, "you were gone, all right? Vi hadn't heard from you in four years. That's a long time. A long time. For all she knew, you weren't ever coming back. According to Henderson, Vi did what she thought was best for you and for the Rocking H."

"And for her friendly and oh-so-helpful neighbor? What all *were* you helping her out with, by the way?" The implication was as ugly as it was absurd. She was ashamed as soon as the words were out. But this was her life they were talking about. This was her home he had the potential to take away. And she was scared.

"Because you don't know me, you don't know how ridiculous that question is. But you did know Vi. And what you just implied is an insult to her memory."

He was right on both counts. She didn't like herself much for saying it, let alone thinking it, but right now she liked him even less. "I guess this explains why you've been so willing to do the work around the place. I thought it was personal—and here it was fiscal. It all benefited you financially."

He gave her a weary look. "You don't get it, do you? If you stay here, we're partners. I don't want to be your partner. I don't need the hassle. I don't need the headache and I don't think you need or want it, either. But if you sell—"

"If I sell, you get the Rocking H for thirty percent less than market. Nice deal."

"No deal. I'm not buying. Let me repeat that. I'm not buying. You sell, you get full market price because I'm not going to be among the bidders. Now do you understand?"

No. She didn't understand. She didn't understand any of this.

"Sell it, Susannah. Take the money and run."

She felt very weary suddenly, leached of her anger, left only with defeat. "I'm tired of running."

"Then use the money and find someplace you don't feel like running away from."

She closed her eyes, shook her head.

"Take a few days to think about it," he said, sounding as weary as she felt. "I can suggest a couple of realtors who can broker the sale for you. At least talk to them. Get a feel for what kind of cash you're looking at here. Trust me. You'll feel better about this when you see a dollar figure."

"A dollar figure," she restated numbly. "You're right about one thing. I don't know you, but you don't know me either if you think money is going to make up for losing my home."

A muscle in his jaw worked. "Just let it settle, all right?"

When she said nothing, he leaned forward, his eyes earnest. "Go home. Get some rest. And think about it. I'll talk to you again tomorrow."

There didn't seem to be anything else to say. She rose, headed for the door, then stopped, but couldn't look at him. "You could do that to me? If I said no, I'm not willing to sell, could you opt to sell anyway? You know it would force me to do the same. There's no way I could come up with the money to buy your half. You'd force me to leave? Take my home away from me?"

Her breath lodged in her throat as she waited. A long, tense moment passed before she found the nerve to turn and face him. She could hear her own heartbeat, see the tension stiffen his shoulders when, without a word or a backward glance, he rose from the table and walked out of the kitchen.

On the drive home, Susannah could still hear the echo of his boot steps on the worn wooden floors as he walked away. For long moments after he left her, she'd stood there, numb and aching before she'd finally let herself out, walked to her Blazer and driven home.

She'd wanted to make him answer her, yet fear of what his answer would be kept her from going after him and pressing the issue.

"Would you do that to me, Travis Dean?" she whispered as she pulled up in front of the house. "If I refuse to leave, would you force the sale of the Rocking H?

"I don't want to leave here, Sooner," she said as the collie met her by the back door. She walked into the house to the den. The dog trailed at her side, rested her chin on Susannah's leg when she sat down at the desk. "I'm finally home. I want to stay."

Home. It was what she'd been searching for all this time. She just hadn't been smart enough to know it. Now she did and she didn't want to be anywhere else.

In desperation, she read the letter and the stipulations of the will again. Then she called the number of the law firm on the letterhead.

Fifteen minutes later, she hung up the phone and accepted, with chilling finality, that she and her baby were at Travis Dean's mercy.

She went to bed early and despite her worry over what would happen next, she slept. Because she was tired. Because she was depressed. Because she needed to shut off her mind. When she awoke at seven the next morning, she lay on the bed in her old downstairs bedroom off the hall behind the stairs and tried to figure out what she was going to do.

"Nothing," she said aloud as she sat up and swung her feet to the floor. Because there was nothing to do. She couldn't subject herself and her unborn child to any more tension. So, she'd do her best to block it out. She was staying; her decision was made. Now she had to wait for Travis to make his.

She forced herself to eat breakfast, got a dose of supplement down Sooner and then gathered the wash she'd forgotten in her anger and had left out on the line all night. When everything was folded and put away, she wandered down to the barn.

Must and hay and animal scents surrounded her as she opened the door and stepped inside. So familiar, so comforting. How many times had she run down here as a little girl to play with the calico kittens in the mow, to watch her father trim hooves, to help him feed the horses?

A soft nicker greeted her. The bay mare was round as a barrel and restless with the weight and the boredom as Susannah slipped into her stall. "Guess there's no question about who's going to deliver first, is there, Sissy girl?

"Ah, so that's why he's got you stalled, instead of running in the pasture with the other mares," she said after checking her bag. The waxy plugs on the tips of the mare's teats were sure signs she would deliver within a few days.

"How about a little scratch and tickle to take your mind off the wait?" she murmured to her dad's favorite horse and dame of several of the babies who were now working horses on the Rocking H. Going to work with a currycomb, she gave the mare a gentle grooming.

It was close to ten by the time she wandered back to the house trying to shake the feeling of being at loose ends. In spite of all her good intentions, worry started niggling away at her again.

Just yesterday, as she'd sorted laundry and made lists in her head, she'd had direction and purpose and hope. Now she had someone else calling the shots for her. Someone who didn't like her and didn't want anything to do with her. Someone who had evidently come over at the crack of dawn, done her chores and lit out like a fast breeze to avoid seeing her.

Could she believe him? Could she believe he'd had nothing to do with forging the terms of Vi's will? Could she count on what she had decided was an intrinsic goodness in him to not throw her out on her ear? At least she'd thought she'd discovered goodness until she'd opened the letter and read the will.

All of those questions drove home the point that she really knew nothing about him. Nothing but what she'd seen in the past two days and frankly, she was more confused now than when she'd first met him.

She stared at the phone for a long time before she picked it up and dialed.

"Clarence, hi," she greeted her father's old fore-man when he answered on the second ring. "It's Su-sannah."

"Well, hey, honey. How you doing over there?"

She smiled into the receiver, the affection in his

voice warming her. "I'm fine, Clarence. How's it going with you? And Martha?"

"Goin' about as good as it can for two old fogies, I s'pose," he answered with a grin in his voice. "Thought we might see you at the Fourth-of-July celebration in town."

Fourth of July. She'd forgotten all about it.

"Reckon you had other things on your mind, though," he added quietly.

"More like I lost track of time," she admitted.

"Not as much as you think. The celebration was a couple days early to catch the weekend crowd. It was a doozie of a parade. And Martha purely ohhed and ahhed over them fireworks. Next year. You'll feel more up to celebrating then. So, what can I do for ya, honey?"

She hesitated then decided there was nothing to be done for it, but to ask. "What can you tell me about Travis Dean?"

She was met by a considering silence, then Clarence cleared his throat. "Why, what'd you want to know?" he asked so carefully it sent her senses on alert.

"Anything. Everything."

"Well." Clarence paused again and she could picture him scrunching up his face and tugging on his ear. "The honest truth is, I'm sad to say I don't know nearly as much about him as I should. Haven't been much of a neighbor to him. I do know he was a good neighbor to Vi. Hard worker, she'd told me. Quick with a hand when she needed it. Mighty good with her stock, too, both know-how and doctoring-wise, even though I understand he was a poodle doc back in California."

"Poodle doc?"

"Oh, you know. Had some fancy veterinary practice and took care of them rich, pampered canines and the like back in San Diego. Made lots of money doing it, too, leastwise that's what Trav's granddaddy tells me. We talk, you know, me and Charlie."

It occurred to her as Clarence rambled on that she had asked Travis the day of Vi's funeral if he was a vet and he'd neatly skirted her question. The obvious dodge on his part only increased her curiosity.

"I, for one, was real glad to hear he was taking over for Charlie and there was still gonna be a Dean on the Lazy D," Clarence continued, "when for a while there, it looked like some hoity-toity development company was gonna buy it and stick up a slug of them getaway places for the rich and famous. Dern fools, wantin' to break up good grazing land.

"Anyway, no matter what else they say about him, he did a good thing when he took over for his granddaddy a few years ago."

One comment among the many reached out and grabbed her by the throat. "No matter what else they say about him?" Susannah repeated when Clarence wound down. "What do they say about him?"

Another uncomfortable silence passed. "Oh, well now, honey, I'm not one to buy into gossip. And I'm not one to spread it. 'Specially the mean kind like was goin' 'round 'bout him. That talk's settled down now, though. And if it really happened, it was before he come here so it's all in the past. I always wondered if there was ever anything to it in the first place or if it was just ignorant folks yapping their jaws to hear themselves talk."

"Clarence," she persisted, her grip on the receiver

tightening, "if there's something I should know about him—"

"Whoa now, girl," he cut in. "I shoulda never brought up that ugly business. Now you got your shorts in a twist and it's probably over nothin'. All you need to know about the man is that he was a good friend to your stepmomma and that Del Brooks thinks he walks on water and makes it rain. Those are two pretty good endorsements in my book."

Okay. So she wasn't going to pry any information out of Clarence. She tried another angle. "He and Vi got to be pretty good friends the way it sounds."

"Yeah, they did and that there was a nice thing that happened, the two of them finding each other. Vi was pretty lonesome out there on her own. The way I heard it, they sort of bumped into each other scouting cows that first spring when Travis took over. There'd been a late snow and she'd found Trav knee-deep in a snow-filled gully helping a sickly little newborn calf. He saved the little critter and their friendship sort of grew from there.

"Yeah," he said, more to himself than to her, "being he's a bit of a loner, folks were kind of surprised he and Vi made a connection, but there it was anyway. She taught him what she knew of ranchin' and he lent her a hand with the heavy work."

"Do you—" She paused, not wanting to ask this outright, but not seeing another way. "Do you think he ever…took advantage of her to win her friendship and her trust?"

"Took advantage? Why, truth to tell, if anything, Vi took advantage of him. I mean, I don't blame her and all. It's hard work for a woman. So yeah, she took advantage of his strength and his back and his vet know-how.''

''And what did he get out of it?''

''Well, I always figured he got the same thing she did. A friend. Plus, darlin', you might have forgot.'' He chuckled. ''Your stepmomma was one mighty fine cook.

''Say, what's all this about, anyway? You worried about whether or not you can trust him? Has he done something? Something that's spooked you?''

''No.'' She didn't want to get into the will and its conditions with Charlie. Neither did she want to get into the strange message from Vi. ''He hasn't done anything. In fact, he's been doing all the work around here.''

''Then forget about what did or didn't happen in his past and thank him. And feed him. He's a big man. I know all I want to know about the workin's of a bachelor's kitchen from before I married my Martha.'' He chuckled again. ''It ain't purty.''

''I'll remember that.''

''Susannah,'' he said after a silent moment passed, ''you got questions about Travis Dean, you ask him, okay? It's the only fair way. What I know of him tells me he'll answer you true.''

''You're right,'' she agreed. ''I'm sorry I put you in a bad position.''

''Oh, shoot now, don't be goin' there. Nobody puts me anywhere I don't want to be. You sure you're okay over there by yourself? You want to come over for a snack or something? Martha made one fine strawberry rhubarb pie today. There's some left, I think. Martha? There some of that pie left?''

"No, but thanks. I'm fine, Clarence. I'll drop by one of these days. Say hi to Martha for me."

"You just call any time, Susannah. Our door's always open to you."

After she'd hung up, she didn't know whether she felt better or worse about Travis. She thought back to the funeral and the luncheon at the house afterward. She'd noticed how the neighbors had regarded him. They'd kept their distance. He'd done the same.

"What didn't Clarence want to tell me?" she asked Sooner and stroked the dog's head where it lay on her lap.

Questions. She'd come home for answers and all she was getting was questions. Could she trust Travis Dean? Did she want to stay on at the Rocking H when her only option was as his partner? And would he even give her that option?

"I don't want to be your partner."

That was what he'd said. Not, I *won't* be your partner. He'd had the opportunity to tell her flat-out no and he hadn't taken it.

It was a technicality that gave her a glimmer of hope, because right now it appeared to be the only hope she had of staying on at the Rocking H. It wasn't much to bank on. She needed an absolute, but it didn't look like she was going to get it.

On a deep breath, she stared out the window, past the barn to the foothills that transitioned to towering granite peaks miles in the distance. Wasn't it a sad commentary that Travis Dean's silence and her hope was all she had to hang on to? And wasn't it ironic that she'd come back to the Rocking H because she'd needed to prove to herself she didn't require anyone but herself to survive?

Over the past four years, her pride, her hopes, her dreams had been stomped on, ripped apart and shredded more times than she could count—all by the men she had relied on to be what she'd needed. None of them had ever been. None would ever be. She'd finally figured that out, had promised herself it would never happen again. Yet here she was, forced to depend on still another man to decide her future for her—and this one didn't even pretend to like her as the others had.

Dragging her gaze away from the window and the sight of everything she might lose, she walked to the fridge and poured a glass of milk. Niggling away in the back of her mind were the questions Clarence had raised about Travis Dean's past.

"Is it a little too coincidental," she wondered aloud as Sooner watched her from a rug by the door, "that he'd become close to Vi and now that she's gone, the least he stands to inherit is half of a very valuable ranch?"

Wanting to steer clear of that possible connection, she drained her glass, rinsed and set it in the sink. Unable to stop herself, she walked straight to her bedroom. She opened the drawer where she'd hidden the decoded note from Vi and reread it, her mind caught again and again by one passage.

"…fate is warning me to leave Colorado, to leave the country for someplace where I will be safe. Safe from what, I cannot tell you as that knowledge could place you in jeopardy as well and I would do anything to keep you from harm…."

She sank down on the bed. Who was Vi trying to be safe from?

She didn't want to think it was Travis, dismissed

the idea out of hand as ludicrous. Yet, if the note was to be believed, Vi had felt threatened by someone. A cold chill ran down her spine. She didn't want to believe he had anything to do with Vi's death, but she'd heard talk at the funeral. He'd been the first at the scene. Another coincidence? Just like it was a coincidence he had a past that kept the locals at a wary distance?

She tried to shake off her heightening sense of unease as she went about her business the rest of the day. But it stayed with her, unsettling, uncomfortable, making her jump at the slightest noise, making her stay in the house that night when Travis pulled up in her lane, walked straight to the barn and did the chores.

She watched him leave from a darkened kitchen, hugging her arms around herself. And she was considering the possibility of having this man as a partner?

Her uncertainty and her fears and her doubt continued to swirl around her as she went to bed and kept circling back to the car wreck. Sheriff Brooks thought there was no chance of Vi's death being deliberate. Vi's coded message suggested he was wrong. But whom had Vi been afraid of?

She tried not to let it, but the answer kept twisting back to Travis Dean. That night the gun lay beside her on the mattress, instead of on the floor. She felt foolish and frazzled and yet a little safer for the cold weight beneath her hand until finally she slept the sleep of the dead.

She slept twelve hours. She hadn't realized how exhausted she was. When she awoke the next morning, she felt amazingly refreshed and renewed. She also had a new perspective, she realized as she dressed in loose blue shorts and a bright red T-shirt and made herself a healthy breakfast.

She sat at the kitchen window, watching a bald eagle drift on the mountain currents and made herself let go of the worries that had weighed her down since she'd returned to the Colorado ranch.

It wasn't good for the baby for her to keep worrying over Vi's death, making more out of a note that was probably written years ago while Vi herself was dealing with her grief. It wasn't good for the baby to try to outguess Travis Dean's motives and his final decision on whether or not he was willing to give a partnership a try.

She couldn't do anything about any of it anyway. And she'd decided to trust Clarence's opinion. Which meant she would trust that Travis didn't have anything to do with Vi's death. It just seemed right.

"Proactive," she announced to Sooner after she'd coaxed the supplement down her when she'd turned up her nose at her breakfast again. "That's what I need to be. And positive. That's why I came home. That's what this is all about."

She got in her Blazer and headed for town. She hadn't planned on turning up pregnant or having Jason walk out when she told him. She hadn't planned on Vi dying, or Sooner not eating, or possibly losing the ranch. And there hadn't been a thing she could have done to stop any of it. She couldn't stop what was or was not going to happen in the future, either.

But she could influence it a little bit, she decided as she pulled up in front of the doctor's office. If a partnership was the only way she could keep the

Rocking H, then she'd have to show her potential partner she was an asset, not a liability.

"And would a partner really be such a bad deal?" she reasoned, looking for the upside as she left the doctor's office with an appointment booked for next week. Someone to share the expenses and the work? Someone who knew the operation and had an investment in what was important to her?

It obviously wasn't what he had in mind. But with some give and take—probably most of it on her part—it could work. If she could trust him. Bottom line: She had no choice but to trust him.

She headed for the grocery story, bought fresh fruit and vegetables and milk for herself, several cans of dog food for Sooner and some plant food for the garden that was neglected and struggling.

Then that night, as she sat down to her supper, she decided her positive attitude was working. The best of all possible things happened. Her eyes filled with tears of relief and joy as she watched Sooner wander over to her bowl, sniff, then eat like there was no tomorrow.

Trav had just stepped out of the shower when the phone rang. He considered letting it ring, but at the last minute wrapped a towel around his hips and stalked into the bedroom.

He snagged the portable receiver off the nightstand. "'Lo."

"Travis?"

"Susannah?" All senses snapped to attention at the tension in her voice. She was crying. Or trying not to. The hand he was forking through his damp hair stopped, fell to his side. "What's wrong?"

"It's Sooner."

He swore under his breath, picturing the worst. "I'll be right there."

"No, wait!"

He paused, trying to decide if she was talking around tears or laughter.

"It's okay. She's okay. She ate. She ate her supper!"

He let out a long breath of relief. "Well, it's about time."

"She's going to be okay now, isn't she?"

Guarded hope undercut her happiness and prompted him to reassure her. "Yeah. She's going to be just fine."

"Well, I...I just wanted you to know."

"Thanks. Thanks for calling."

"Travis?"

"Yeah?"

A long silence passed. "I'm sorry I blew up at you the other day. I... The will was a shock. That's my only excuse."

He could see her. Tears brimming in those big eyes, her hands clutched around the receiver, relief and elation feeding color to her cheeks and easing some of the weight from her shoulders. And he could see himself drawing her into his arms.

"I imagine I'd have had the same reaction if it had been me," he said and before he said something else—something like, You want me to come over?—he said goodbye.

He stared at the receiver before dropping it back in the cradle. With absent motions, he scrubbed the towel over his chest, tossed it in the general direction of the shower then dragged on a clean pair of gray sweats.

The house was quiet. Too quiet, he thought and wondered why it bothered him tonight when solitude had been his sanctuary for the past three years. He wandered into the living room, grabbed the remote and punched on the TV. Then he sat down in his chair, listened without really hearing as the newscaster droned over the on-screen images of floodwaters in Missouri, then switched to a chemical spill in upstate New York.

Life, or something like it, went on across the world. Everything and nothing changed—like his own life. He got up. He worked. He went to bed. Simple. Basic. Enough.

Or it had been until a few days ago.

The news scene changed again. This time an ambulance careened through an Atlanta street. But in his mind's eye he revisited the image of Susannah smiling through tears at a dog that had finally decided life was worth living.

He'd known Sooner was either going to come around or she wasn't. Or it could be the dog's way of saying she was ready to trust again. She was trusting that Susannah wouldn't leave her as Vi had.

Trust. Small word. Big issue.

And he didn't know why he was thinking about it. Or why he was still thinking about Susannah. He just plain didn't get it. And he didn't know how to deal with it.

What he did know was that regardless of his preoccupation with Susannah Hobson and the things she made him think about, the things she made him feel, there could never be anything between them. She'd get to thinking about what she stood to gain if she sold out and she'd realize what she'd lose if she didn't. He wouldn't even have to convince her. She'd come to the conclusion herself and be gone in less than a month.

He was banking on it. For his peace of mind. For the straightforward reason that he felt too much when he was around her. And even when he wasn't.

It wasn't rational. He'd just met her. But there it was anyway. Like an ache that wouldn't let up. Like a need that wouldn't be satisfied. Tough. He may want her, but he couldn't have her. If this business with the will wasn't enough of a reason to keep his distance, their age difference was. So was the fact that she carried another man's baby. A man who, regardless of what she'd said, may just sashay back into her life and decide he wanted to be a daddy once he found out about the money she'd pocket when she sold the Rocking H.

And then there was the bigger truth. If he took her to bed it would be for one reason. He'd be using her. For his own pleasure, out of selfishness. Sex was the sum total of what he could offer a woman. Even if he felt he was finally ready to let go of the anger, he was still a long way from having anything else in him to give.

Elena had seen to that. And he had just enough sense of fair play left in him to make sure he didn't do to Susannah what Elena had done to him.

He only knew of one way to make sure he stuck by his conviction. Until she made up her mind to bail, he was staying the hell away from her.

Seven

The next few days passed in an insulated blur for Susannah. Once she'd reaffirmed the necessity of shedding her guilt and her worries and just let happen what was going to happen, she experienced all the joy, all the sense of homecoming and peace she'd dreamed of during the past four months.

In the mornings the air was like crystal. Clear, pure, glittering with summer sunlight. The jagged mountains flanking the valley stood like sentinels. Tall, proud, constant. She loved it here. She'd forgotten how much. She loved the scent of the second cutting of alfalfa Travis had mowed yesterday. She loved watching the horses and the softness of their coats, the clarity of the days and the cool, honest darkness of the nights.

She loved the feel of the damp earth in her hands as she bent over the little patch of garden she'd slowly nursed back to good health. She'd had leaf lettuce with her dinner last night. The tomatoes were plumping up and the peppers would be ripe in another few weeks. And the flowers—pansies and petunias and impatiens—bloomed, too. Her mother had loved flowers. Vi had known it and planted them every year so Susannah could keep the connection with her mom. Susannah intended to carry on the tradition and refused to let herself dwell on the possibility of Travis not giving her the opportunity.

It was a little late to be planting yet more flowers, but she didn't care. It was a little late for Sissy to be foaling, too, but Clarence had told her she hadn't settled when they'd bred her last May so they'd waited to breed her back. Each morning she awoke and ran to the barn, but so far, still no new baby.

There were new kittens in the mow, though—little calicos with fuzzy fur and pinched little mews that made her smile and snuggle them to her breast whenever she brought the pair some of mommas extra milk.

She sat back on her heels at the edge of the garden, rubbing her hard, puffy abdomen. She grinned when Sooner waddled over to her and plopped down with a grunt. "This is just one green, fertile, reproductive summer, isn't it, girl? And you're getting close, too, aren't you, sweetie?" She wiped her damp hands on the soiled legs of her jeans and patted Sooner's head. "Just think about those pretty babies," she soothed and remembered when Sooner was a baby herself.

She'd been seventeen when her dad had brought the little ball of fur and button eyes home. "What will we name her?" she'd asked, filled with excitement as she'd watched the inquisitive puppy scurry around on the kitchen floor then promptly stop, squat and water the linoleum.

Vi had shaken her head, cleaned up the little puddle and lifted the puppy in her arms. "Guess we'll have to call her Sooner because she'd sooner do her business in here than wait until she gets outside."

The name had stuck, even though Sooner was a

quick learner. She'd practically housebroken herself once she'd figured out the way of things.

"Come on, girl, let's see if we can figure out the lawn mower." She'd taken over morning and evening chores. She hadn't asked, she'd just done it, and she hadn't seen much of her potential partner since. "Not a reason in the world I can't do a little more around here to earn my keep."

She was on her way to the garage when she spotted Travis's truck out in the field. It had been days since she'd seen anything other than his backside leaving. She checked her watch. It was close to noon. She considered the heat, considered his recurrent disappearing acts and made an abrupt turn toward the house. Ten minutes later, she had a picnic basket filled with iced lemonade, thick sandwiches, chips and a container of oatmeal raisin cookies.

"Let him try to run away from this," she said with a grin as she helped Sooner into the passenger seat of the Blazer and set out across the field. "The man's got to eat, right? And I never met one yet who could resist lemonade in July."

Suddenly, she felt like she had a game plan. Oh, she knew he had one, too. He figured he'd ignore her and she'd go away. Well, two could play that game only she wasn't going to ignore him exactly. She was going to ignore the fact that they were at cross purposes. If she didn't talk about the problem, maybe it would just go away. It had worked for almost a week now, maybe she could stretch it into a month or a year or even longer than that. If she just had the patience to keep her mouth shut.

Trav heard her coming before he saw her—and by then it was too late. He stared at the wire cutters in his hand, stared off toward the mountains, then let out a resigned breath. He'd known he couldn't dodge her forever. He'd just hoped that by the time he had to face her again, she'd be ready to leave and he'd be past the gut-knotting compulsion to drag her into his arms and kiss her until they were clawing at each other's clothes.

"Knot-head," he muttered under his breath and, rounding his truck, threw the wire cutters angrily into the toolbox. "Wing nut," he grunted, set his mouth into a grim line and waited for her to drive up. "Randy-boy."

He muttered a crude expletive. There wasn't going to be any running away from her today.

"Hi," she said brightly as she let herself and then Sooner out of the Blazer.

He gave her a grudging nod, which for some reason she seemed to find amusing, instead of intimidating.

"Thought you might be hungry. And I'm sure you can use something to drink," she added, opening the rear door of the Blazer and reaching for a picnic basket.

Her shorts were way too short and her legs still way too long, Trav thought as he watched in silence through narrowed eyes.

"Hot," she said as she hefted the basket up beside him where he stood, his arms crossed over his chest, his hands tucked under his armpits, leaning against the open tailgate.

"Whew. Darn hot," she added for emphasis as she slid the basket into the truck bed, planning on using it as a makeshift picnic table.

He grunted in response. It was hot, all right. And getting hotter.

She smiled again. "Haven't seen much of you lately."

"Been busy."

"Me, too," she said brightly and evidently chose to ignore his less-than-welcoming responses. She backed up to the tailgate and, bracing her hands on either side of her ribs, attempted to hike herself up. She got nowhere.

The failed attempt made her laugh. "Oh, man. I knew I'd packed on a few pounds, but this is ridiculous."

He didn't feel like laughing. While the rounding of her abdomen was obvious, it was still slight. Any pounds she'd added were concentrated there—and in her breasts. She looked ripe and lush. With her hands levered up behind her that way, her breasts pushed tightly against her little tank top. He could see the outline of her nipples against the stretchy cotton as she gave it another try.

"Hold the hell still," he grumbled, and in desperation, he shucked his gloves, wedged his hands under her arms and lifted, depositing her gently on the tailgate. Her hands flew involuntarily to his biceps to steady herself.

He made a mistake then. He didn't let go. He just stood there, holding her, smelling the summer heat of her. Feeling the softness of her against the heels of his hands where they pressed against the outer swell of her breasts. Experiencing the heat of her where his hips were cushioned by the smooth skin of her inner thighs.

Her hands, long-fingered and elegant, still gripped

his arms, as if she, too, was held captive by the moment.

It had been a long time since he'd touched a woman, since he'd been touched by one. Even this slight contact stirred memories, conjured images of soft hands seeking in the dark, lingering, softly stroking.

He closed his eyes and when he opened them again, he made another mistake. He stared dead ahead, where the gold chain lay against her chest. Sunlight glinted off the gold as he followed the line of it down, down, where it disappeared between the valley of her breasts. He swallowed, shifted his attention to her mouth.

Wrong. Ripe as peaches, glistening with clear gloss, her lips were parted in surprise and not much more than a breath away from his. All he had to do was lean in, just a little, and he could taste her. Taste the breathlessness of her shock, feel the texture of her lush lower lip, experience the smooth glide of his tongue over hers. All he had to do was push her back on the flat bed, crawl up there beside her...

"Um."

Her tentative murmur snapped him back to sanity. He drew his hands away and stepped back as if he'd been burned.

"Thanks," she said, her voice husky and low, edgy with uncertainty and tempered with something that could have been anticipation. She reached up with an unsteady hand and dragged a fall of hair away from her face.

Good God, Trav thought.

"Oh...damn," she swore on a quick intake of breath and jackknifed forward, clutching at her calf.

Alarm shot through him like a whip. He pinched her chin in his hand, made her look at him. "What? What's wrong?"

Her face contorted with pain. "Cramp. Oh, darn. Darn! Darn! Darn!"

He shoved her hands aside and lifted her foot to his chest. "You've got no business out in this heat," he grumbled as he whipped off her sandal and pressed the flat of her bare foot against his sternum. With gentle pressure on her knee, he forced her leg straight and tipped her toes up. With quick exploration of his fingers, he found the knot and began kneading.

"Oh, man. That bites."

"Try to relax."

She managed a strangled laugh as she eased back, supporting her weight on her elbows. "Easy for you to say," she ground out as her head fell back, her jaw clenched tight.

He concentrated on working the cramped muscle, keeping his head down, his mind on his task. Later, he would relive the feel of her long leg in his hands. Later, he would remember the texture of her silken skin, the supple resistance of muscle and bone. Much later, he would lie in bed, hard for her, aching for her, and damn himself for a fool.

Finally, he felt her relax and chanced meeting her eyes.

"Better?"

She let out a breath through puffed cheeks. "Much. Thanks."

"You seeing a doctor?" He continued to massage her calf, making sure the knot was worked out.

"I have an appointment at the clinic in Walden

tomorrow afternoon. And I was seeing one regularly in Sheridan. I'm fine. Everything's fine.''

"How often are you getting these cramps?"

She sat up again, winced a little when he slowly lowered her leg.

"Toes up," he ordered and when she complied, repeated, "How often?"

"Now and then. Mostly at night. They'll set you straight up in bed, let me tell you."

He didn't want to think about her anywhere near a bed, laying back in the throes of passion. It was bad enough he'd just seen her reclined in the throes of pain. He turned away, found her sandal on the ground and handed it to her.

"I'm okay. Really," she said, slipping it on. "I've done a lot of reading. Cramps are pretty normal for this stage of my pregnancy."

"Well, like I said, this heat doesn't help. You shouldn't be out here."

Without another word, he wedged one arm under her thighs, the other under her shoulder and around her back and lifted her out of the truck bed. "Can you drive?" he asked as he carried her to the Blazer.

"For heaven's sake, it was a charley horse. I'm not going into labor."

"But you *are* getting out of the sun. Now, can you drive?"

"Yes. I can drive," she sputtered. "I can walk, too. You know, if you sprain your back playing macho man, it's going to ruin your reputation."

He almost laughed. If she only knew about his reputation. But he kept on walking until he reached the driver's side of her Blazer. "I'll get Sooner and follow you."

"But your lunch…"

He'd already turned away. He couldn't afford to stand there and let her see the effect she had on him. If just touching her, just worrying about her had cranked him to this instant state of arousal, he didn't want to know how tightly he'd wind if he'd done what he'd wanted to do just now and kissed the protest right off her lips.

He really didn't want to know.

The authoritative Mr. Dean didn't hang around long. He made sure she got to the house, shoved a glass of water in her hand and ordered her to stay out of the sun. She made sure he took a couple of sandwiches and some cookies and lemonade with him.

He was irritating and bossy and…kind of sweet, she thought in retrospect, the way he'd fussed and stewed and grumbled. It had been a long time since anyone had cared enough about her to get cranky.

And it had been a long time since a man had looked at her the way he'd looked at her when he'd lifted her effortlessly onto the tailgate of his truck. At first, she'd thought she'd imagined it. But then…well then, she'd not only seen it, she'd felt it. Hunger. And she'd felt her own answering need. She touched a hand to the side of her breast, where his hand had burned through her top and her bra.

She still didn't know if she was relieved or disappointed that her leg cramp had ended that moment. She knew what she should be—thankful to have escaped a kiss that would have led straight to disaster.

She couldn't afford to get involved with Travis Dean. Didn't want to risk another failed relationship that would only end in disappointment.

"Listen to yourself. Talking about making mountains of molehills. So you shared a look. So he fussed over you. He probably didn't feel anything but grudging responsibility."

And he still held the key to her future.

To take her mind off when or what he would finally decide about the partnership, Susannah went back to the computer to study the ranch records she'd found the other day.

She didn't get past the Secrets file. For the past two weeks, she'd forced all thoughts of Vi's note and its implications out of her mind. Tonight, though, her defenses were low. She walked to her bedroom, dragged the note out of her bureau and read it.

The thoughts and doubts and speculation started swirling around again. She knew she was verging on obsessing over it, but couldn't get it out of her head. Neither did she know what she was looking for. Something, anything to either dispel the notion Vi's death had been steeped in foul play or to cement her suspicions into fact.

Treasure. The word kept jumping out at her. Twice, Vi had mentioned the word. "Treasure always what we shared.... Remember always the treasure that is life."

Like the word secret, treasure was an intrinsic part of their past together. Was she making more of it than it was—or was it yet another veiled message within a message?

The notion struck her so hard and fast, she felt the blood drain from her head. She breathed deep and steadied herself. When the dizzying rush eased, she slowly rose and walked out of the den, then she stared up the length of the open staircase.

Treasure.

One of Vi's favorite places to hide little treasures for Susannah to find lay behind a loose board at the bottom of the attic stairs. Could something possibly be hidden there now?

Slowly, she climbed the fourteen steps to the second story. At the top of the landing she stopped, then moved forward on leaden feet, bypassing the three closed doors leading to bedrooms. Straight ahead was the attic door.

With an unsteady hand, she clutched the knob and turned it. It turned hard, but finally gave to the sighing complaint of ancient hinges. For a long moment, she stood there, looking up into the shadowy darkness as dust motes danced across a slant of sunlight filtering in through a dusty dormer. Finally, she looked down, and with the same sense of foreboding as she'd approached the storm cellar the night that now seemed so long ago, she knelt and skimmed her fingers along the panel under the bottom step.

Even though she was prepared for it, it startled her when the board came loose at her gentle tug. How many times had she found a little treasure hidden here? A magic decoder ring. A page of stickers. Her favorite sweet treat.

But it wasn't a child's toy that awaited her in the secret hiding place today. And it wasn't with a child's brimming excitement that she reached into the hidden compartment. She knew before she touched her fingers to the package. Something much more important than a pretty ribbon for her hair awaited her there.

It wasn't an envelope this time. It was a box approximately eight inches wide, eleven inches long and

three inches deep. It could have once held computer
paper. It could still. But somehow she didn't think so.

Holding her breath, she lifted the lid—and found
paper after all. Page after page filled with the same
type of coded message Vi had used in the other note.

She closed her eyes, hugged the pages to her breast
and prepared herself for what was about to be revealed.

She lost track of time then. She worked past sunset
and into the night as Vi's words—a diary or journal
of sorts—dragged her into a story so incredible, she
couldn't help but wonder if it was fiction. A niggling
sense of dread, however, told her otherwise. Told her
that everything written on these pages was the absolute truth, as not only Vi's story, but her emotions
poured from the pages.

The work was tedious and slow. But now she had
no doubt. The journal that she decoded letter by letter
held the key—not only to those unknown corners of
Vi's life, but to the mystery of her death.

Susannah was half asleep as, one last time, she
scanned the few pages of the many she'd managed to
decode. Bits and pieces of Vi's life drifted up through
the murky waters of her past, compelling her to keep
going, to unravel what Vi had deemed necessary to
record in code.

In an undated entry she wrote:

*It's hard to believe I was ever so young. It's hard
to believe I was ever Violet Vaughn, that I'd lived
another life before I came to Colorado. But it's suddenly important that I record my thoughts. To what
purpose? I'm not sure. But I'm compelled to do so
and that tells me it's important to get this all down.*

Where to begin? When everything changed, I guess, in 1963. I was nineteen. I'd been full of dreams, excited about my future. It was a difficult time in our country. The Vietnam conflict—the war that was not a war—was killing our young men, dividing our nation. In retrospect, I feel guilt over my self-absorbed preoccupation with my own life.

I must, however, give myself a little latitude here, remember that I was still very young. And it wasn't that I was self-absorbed in a selfish way. It was just that I hadn't anticipated this. Suddenly, I'm finding it hard to speak of it, even as I write this down, even knowing my journals may never be found. I'm alone again now. Dale has been gone for almost three months. I miss him; I miss Susannah. So sad. So determined to run away from her pain....

Susannah had to stop, blink back tears as she realized these journals had been written shortly after she'd left the Rocking H four years ago. Vi's loneliness poured from the pages. Steeling herself against what the complete text would reveal, she forced herself to go on.

But I digress. I do that a lot these days. My thoughts scatter, regroup, then fade away again. I was thinking today of when I was a little girl. Georgia peaches, my daddy used to call me and my sister. I loved them all so, Momma and Daddy and Iris. And then one day they were gone. I never knew the name of the drunk who hit them. Eleven-year-olds don't remember names. I do remember the pain, like a sucking hole draining the life out of me, too. When they told me someone from up in the hills, stoned on home brew, had cut across the center line and ended his life as well as life as I'd known it. I remember the pain as if it were yesterday.

I'd been on a sleepover with a friend. How hard it had been for her mother to tell me. I remember feeling bad for her. Isn't that odd? My life had just fallen apart and I felt sorry for her.

I was to have no one then, no family. No aunts or uncles to take me in. For the first time in my life I was alone. Little did I know I would find myself in the same situation over and over again as the years passed. But I survived, perhaps because even as a child, I'd been very precocious. That was according to my father. He used to beam when he said it, though, and I'd known he was proud of both my intellect and my rebel streak. It didn't take long, however, for me to learn to hide anything about myself that would draw attention. Moving from foster family to foster family, I grew up fast. Some families were loving; some were merely bearable and others showed me the cruel depravity of man at his worst. I learned to lock my bedroom door at night—when I had a door to lock—to hide anything remotely feminine about myself. I retreated into a world of books, where I could escape the nightmare that my life had become.

Science and biology. Ah. What great escapes! What great adventures! I'll never forget Vivian Greene. Goodness. I haven't thought of her in such a long time. Such a caring teacher. She was responsible for helping me secure a scholarship to Emory University in Atlanta, although she insisted it was my doing. I didn't tell her it was no difficult charge to earn straight A's when all I did was study. Dating was out of the question. I couldn't draw attention to myself. I'd learned— Well, I've already alluded to what I'd learned.

Did it mean I didn't fantasize at night about a white knight? No. Did it mean I never declared my romantic feelings to some sweet boy who had caught my eye? Yes. That's what it meant. I can smile about it now. At least a little. I was such a bookish little mouse by the time I attended Emory. Oh, but I'm rambling again.

I wanted to talk about Henry. My first true love. Maybe tomorrow night. I'm tired now. And there's so much to do now that Dale is gone. Dale. Sweet, steady Dale. So much to do....

Susannah sat up straight. Henry? Her first love? Of course, Vi had had a life prior to marrying her father, but she'd never thought of her as having another love. More intrigued than ever, she rolled her head on her shoulders, massaged her neck and told herself again to go to bed. But she couldn't. She simply couldn't. Two hours later, she wished she had.

At Emory, for the first time, being alone and on my own was a blessing. It gave me freedom as I'd never experienced before. To expand my horizons, to explore my femininity. Not that I drew much attention from the opposite sex. Not that I wanted their attention. The boys my age were— Well, is there any kind way to say it? No, sadly. They were immature, for the most part on the make. It was the free-love generation and I learned early on that the best things in life were not free.

Again, I'm digressing. As much as I adored college, money was tight for me. I finally found a job cleaning the lab run by one of my professors, Dr. Henry Bloomfield.

Henry Bloomfield. Even as I write this, I find myself

*blushing like a schoolgirl. He was magnificent. He
was brilliant, an acclaimed scientist and the world's
leading authority in genetic engineering. Can you
imagine my nineteen-year-old heart speeding up at
the thought of working near this great man? In this
day and age, genetic engineering is commonplace,
and cloning is a reality. But in the '60s it was considered more science fiction than actual research and
experimentation, but yet, here he was, this exceptional
man forging new paths to discoveries that could
change the course of the world.*

*All that brilliance and such a tragically lost man.
His story was heartbreaking. Perhaps that's one of
the reasons I was so drawn to him. When I heard his
story, I realized we shared a common grief. He'd lost
something, too.*

*Henry had been married to the love of his life.
Their future was so bright. And when news of the
imminent birth of twins arrived, they were ecstatic.
That all changed when the twin boys were born with
congenital heart deformities, the result of mixed-up
signals from a faulty gene. They'd died within hours
of birth despite all efforts to save them.*

*I can't imagine the grief Henry's wife must have
felt. I've since seen pictures of her. She was very
beautiful, but also very fragile. After the death of the
babies, she fell into a deep depression and finally suc-
cumbed. She committed suicide. My heart aches for
her and for Henry even now, all these years later as
I continue to deal with the loss of my own children.*

Susannah swallowed hard, overcome with curiosity
and empathy. *Loss of her own children?* She glanced
at the clock. It was past midnight. She knew she
should go to bed, but she couldn't make herself stop.

Just a few more pages. There were so many. It would take so much time.

Henry was also destroyed by this devastating loss. So much so, he attempted to kill himself. If I hadn't arrived to do my nightly cleaning at the lab when I did, he would have died.

I can still see it so clearly. I walked in and he was pale as death, lying on the cold tile floor with a hypodermic syringe at his side, the fluorescent light already casting his face in a ghastly, yellowed hue. I was terrified!

I'd heard stories of mothers lifting cars off their children to save their lives, of soldiers risking all, performing superhuman feats to save their fallen comrades. I understand now how those anomalies occur. When I saw Henry near death, something primitive and vital swept over me. Do I remember applying mouth-to-mouth? Do I remember screaming for help between breaths? No. It's still a blur. They told me they had to drag me away from him when the paramedics arrived. Again, I don't remember. The only thing I do remember was the ominous sense of his life slipping away and my determination not to let it go.

And I didn't. Henry survived. Despite the fact he'd tried to end his life with a lethal injection. They said it was a miracle. That I had saved him.

The beginning of a love story? Definitely on my part. I was already half in love with him, even though at nineteen most would have dismissed it as infatuation.

But no. It was not the beginning of love—at least not on his part, not at first. Instead, he resented me for not letting him die. His cold rebuff was painful. I was devastated. And even more so when he left Emory for a time to retreat to his childhood home in North Carolina.

I grieved, but Henry healed there at Belle Terre in the antebellum mansion by the ocean, which had been left to him by his parents. At least he'd healed after a fashion and then he made the decision to return to Emory.

All I could think was another chance. I was over-joyed with the news of his return. My heart is beating hard now as I write this and remember. I haven't revisited these memories in such a very long time. Perhaps I don't have the strength I'd thought. It will be difficult to relate what happened next. Little did I know that the path I'd chosen that fateful day when I signed on as his assistant would lead from joy to sorrow, to horrible acts and death.

May God forgive me. I didn't know. I simply didn't know....

Shaken, Susannah stopped, stared beyond the night, beyond the years, and felt for the first time like she was truly meeting Vi. What had she survived, this woman whom her father had loved? And what, in the name of God could she have done that she felt compelled to beg God for forgiveness?

When Henry returned to Emory, I immediately applied for the position of his lab assistant. Oh, he was reluctant to hire me at first. Only years later did he confide in me that my presence reminded him of that horrible day when he'd decided he could no longer go on. It embarrassed him that I'd seen him, that anyone had seen him at such a low point.

I remember I was still so shy, but I remember bungling through some insipid statement. Something like the true low point would have been his loss to the scientific community. And to me. "Because I so admire you. Admire your work," I quickly added, mortified he'd see how infatuated I was with him. He must have looked upon me as a child. And compared to him—he was thirty at the time—I was.

In any event, for a time he insisted he wanted to work with a grad student. But every night, I'd show up to clean as I had for the past several months. And that precocious trait my father had so loved? Well, I found it again. I persisted. I asked questions, showed him how interested I was in his work, proved to him I had the intellect to be of value. In short, I wore him down.

He finally gave in. And, oh, what a victory that was for me. And what a wonder the research turned out to be. Unfortunately, in the end, it was also a horrible, horrible mistake.

What I constantly need to remind myself is that Henry was driven by the purest of motives. His passion wore off on those around him. Not knowing then what I know now, I eagerly signed on for the ride. He was on a mission—and he was magnificent in his fervor. It was the loss of his infant twins that drove him. In his mind, the corner of it that still grieved, he'd decided there was only one way he could cope. Only one way to give new purpose and meaning to the rest of his life.

He dedicated himself to perfecting the human species from the very earliest stages of life so that the race would forever be spared such cruel and random accidents of nature that had stolen his family. Anyone and everyone experiencing his excitement and verve for the project immediately fell under the spell he cast around them.

Perhaps now would be a good time to explain why I, like so many others, was so easily able to overlook the potential for disaster in his plan. You see, it wasn't just that Henry intended to make a genetically perfect child, free of birth defects, inherited diseases and abnormalities. He intended to go beyond perfection on a physical level. He aspired to perfect the entire human design to its ultimate, unlimited potential. He had a dream. A dream of designing babies who would grow to adults with the physical abilities of super-heroes, intellect at genius level with the wisdom and leadership skills and the creative abilities of the world's greatest philosophers, political leaders and artists.

I know. Looking back, thinking it through, I know it sounds insane. Like the work of a madman. But Henry wasn't mad. Henry envisioned his research as a golden opportunity for a perfect human race to live in a perfect society. Within his grasp was the potential for mankind to live free of crime, free of war and disease, to live as one cooperative whole in a cultural and technologically advanced society. Utopia. It was no longer merely an idealized fantasy to him. With the breakthroughs he was making in his research, it was a conceivable reality.

I cannot express the excitement I experienced when I realized the extent of his vision. And I cannot underscore enough that as the years passed and his progress brought us closer to fruition, we were both so optimistic of the potential boon to mankind that we did not see the dark side of his vision. We did not see that such knowledge could be manipulated for evil. We did not know the path we'd chosen would lead to such devastating ends....

Unbelievable, Susannah thought as she straightened and kneaded her lower back of the kinks several hours of decoding had brought. A superior human race? She made herself step back. Maybe this *was* science fiction, after all. Maybe Vi had some secret desire to become a published author. The story was certainly compelling enough—and so far out in left field, Susannah wanted to believe it was all fantasy. An exercise to relieve Vi's mind of loneliness. An escape of sorts, fabricated by a woman alone who had grown weary of the solitude and played mind games with pen and paper to ease the boredom.

This was the same woman who had created a code to entertain a little girl, after all. The same woman who had hidden treasures around the house. The same woman who had loved Susannah's father and put up with Susannah's childish disdain, she reminded herself soberly. She had been a woman gifted with the art of whimsy—but she had not been fanciful. She'd been pragmatic and thoughtful and balanced.

As much as Susannah wanted to believe this story was a figment of Vi's imagination, every instinct she owned told her otherwise. If this story was true, the ramifications were unspeakable. Ruthless individuals would kill to have Professor Bloomfield's secrets.

The thought brought her up short. Vi was dead and the possibility that she may have been murdered only grew in plausibility the further Susannah read. The speculation was more than enough to make her want to get back to her task.

But she couldn't. She simply couldn't read any more, was too fatigued to work at deciphering the coded words. She gathered her notes and the journals and locked them in the bottom drawer of the file cabinet. Then she added the key to the chain she still wore around her neck. As she dragged herself to bed and fell, exhausted, beneath the sheets, the thought crossed her mind that she wished she'd never found the journals. She wasn't sure she wanted to know what happened next. And yet, she knew she wouldn't be able to stop herself from pressing on.

Tomorrow. Tomorrow, when she was rested. Tonight she had to sleep. Tonight, edgy and a little spooked by Vi's ominous words, she grabbed the rifle and took it with her to bed again. It felt as if she'd just closed her eyes when a hard hand gripped her shoulder and shook her awake.

"Susannah!"

She rolled over, then propelled by shock and fear, scrambled to sit up against the headboard. She blinked against harsh daylight and the ice in the eyes of the man who stood by her bed. His broad shoulders filled her vision and sent her pulse rocking. His mouth was as hard and angry as the gun he held in his hand.

Eight

Trav glared at Susannah as she huddled on the bed, clearly struggling to assemble what she was seeing into something she could deal with. She looked scared to death. Fine. He'd been scared, too. Good and scared until he'd found her.

He'd shown up at eight, found a healthy new filly in the barn and after making sure both mother and daughter were fine, he'd cleaned their stall and done the rest of the chores. Then he'd hung around, waiting for a light to come on in the kitchen. He didn't want to talk to her. What he wanted, however, didn't negate the need. They had unfinished business, and ever since yesterday when he'd damn near made a fool of himself over her and kissed her, he'd decided it was time to get it settled.

When nine-thirty rolled around and there was still no sign of life, he'd stalked up the back porch steps and glared through the glass in the kitchen door like a damn peeping Tom. When he'd seen no activity, he'd started to worry in earnest. He'd rapped sharply on the glass pane and when she didn't answer and he found the door locked, fear shifted to panic.

She was pregnant. She was alone. She'd been over-heated yesterday; he'd been concerned she was going to suffer some kind of complication right there in the sun. Even after he'd managed to order her up to the house where she could cool off and get her pins back under her, he'd been concerned. Maybe she'd experienced some delayed stress reaction. Maybe she'd passed out. Lost the baby.

The thought had made him physically ill. He'd retrieved the key Vi always left on the dusty molding above the outdoor frame and let himself inside.

Quiet. It was too quiet, he realized, then stormed through the house looking for her.

He'd found her. Not ill. Not in trouble. But sleeping.

Startled awake, half-covered in tangled sheets, her hair tumbled over her left shoulder, her pale blue nightshirt slid off her right and high on her hip. He should look away. He couldn't. Her panties were white, high-cut and edged in lace. The flesh below the elastic was pale and firm.

Jaw clenched, he finally dragged his eyes to her face. She stared at him from behind a fall of tangled hair and startled blue eyes, whose fear slowly shifted to recognition. And all he could think, all he could feel was a primitive, volatile and gut-deep reaction to all her female softness.

Awareness hit him like a shotgun blast. Awareness of lush, parted lips that trembled slightly. Awareness of her scent. God, he could smell her. Her woman's heat and softness. And he could imagine the warmth of the sheets beneath her, the give of the mattress, the silk of her skin and the fluid strength of her long legs tangled with his.

Some things he didn't have to imagine. The round fullness of her breasts pressed against the stretchy nightshirt; her nipples were taut and clearly outlined against the fabric that molded the shape, the size and the weight of her.

Below her breasts, the slight roundness of her belly reminded him of what he'd forgotten yesterday. Another man's child rested there. The image of his ex-wife—round with a child that wasn't his—hit him like a gut punch.

He glared at Susannah, blamed her for bringing it all back, making him remember, making him want. Worse, making him weak.

He swore under his breath. Why the hell did she have to come back here and stir up memories of something she'd had no part in, but managed to rile just the same? He didn't need her to complicate his life. What he wanted was to be left alone. That was all he wanted.

He wanted to work—alone—and to wear out his body so his mind would shut down at night. Deep, exhausted sleep was his best defense against a lot of old baggage he'd never been able to completely unload.

And he'd been getting there—until she'd shown up with her soulful blue eyes, shadowed with pain, and regarded him with a weary wisdom beyond what someone her age should have experienced. She made him aware that beneath the surface he still had needs; he was still human. He still felt desire.

He dragged his gaze from her eyes to the gun he'd lifted off her bed, and something inside him exploded. He'd like to call it rage. How stupid could she be, dragging out that relic and sleeping with it where she could roll over on it and— Hell, anything could happen.

Yeah, he'd like to call it rage—but deep down he

recognized it as something else. Fear. For her. Hell. He hadn't even wanted to like her and now he was caring about what happened to her.

"What in the hell is wrong with you?" he demanded, taking his anger at himself out on her. "What possible reason could you have to sleep with this gun?"

"Travis." That was all she had to say. Just "Travis," as if she'd finally put it together that she was awake and he wasn't a figment of her imagination. She wouldn't be sitting there if she knew what he was thinking. She'd be running. Running scared and fast and far, instead of blinking at him like a baby owl trying to figure out why he was standing by her bed.

"How—how did you get in here? What are you doing in here?" she amended, dragging the hair back from her face.

For a moment, he couldn't respond. All he could do was stare at the gentle motion of her unbound breasts shifting beneath her nightshirt as she lifted her arm. The unconscious sensuality of the movement set off a blaze of sexual heat that burned through him like a live wire.

"It's going on ten o'clock," he snarled to remind them both that he was angry.

"Ten? Oh. Oh, my."

"And this is how you plan on running your ranch?" He heard the disgust, knew he was being unfair, but couldn't stop himself.

He could see that she was exhausted. Obviously, she hadn't slept. At least not well. Velvet smudges formed beneath her eyes like pale bruises. Her shoulders sagged as she leaned forward, finally gaining the presence of mind to drag the sheet up and over her legs to cover herself.

"I still want to know what you're doing with that gun." He lifted the rifle when he felt himself soften toward her again. He did not want to feel compassion for this woman. Not compassion, not lust. And damn her, she made him feel too much of both.

She stared from the gun to his face, clearly searching for an explanation. When it finally came, it sounded as lame as his trumped-up anger.

"Coyote," she said. "Last night I—I heard a coyote and..."

When she trailed off and shrugged, he angled her a look. "And thought you'd what? Blow his head off in the dark?"

"Scare him into the next county," she bit back, the edge of her temper flaring as she rallied her wits about her.

She was lying. He could see it in the defensive set of her jaw before she averted her eyes, unwilling or unable to hold his gaze.

"There wasn't any coyote, but you got yourself good and spooked, didn't you? You've been back how long? Not even two weeks? And already you're feeling the fear of being out here alone?"

"I'm not afraid of staying by myself."

He stared at her long and hard, at the determined lift of her chin, at the denial that came too fast and too strong.

"Would you mind?" she asked with a vague lift of her hand that clearly showed him the door.

Yeah. He minded. He minded that he'd been standing there way too long and it had taken her to remind him it was past time he got the hell out of her bedroom.

"In case you're interested, Sis had a filly last night." Then he turned and walked away from her and her bed and the erotic images he'd been fighting since he'd found her in it. Sleep-tumbled, tempting. As out of bounds as the original sin.

And God help him, he muttered, as he slammed out the kitchen door and stalked back to the barn. He wanted her.

She'd gotten past the shakes. Gotten past the alarm. Not that she'd really thought he'd shoot her in her own bed, she realized as she dressed and pulled her hair back, securing it with a gold clip at her nape. But for the long moment when she'd hovered somewhere between sleep and shocked awakening, confusion had ruled and she'd thought... Well, she'd seen his scowl, seen her gun in his big hand and thought maybe it was the last thing she'd ever see.

Until she'd seen the hunger in his eyes. She shivered at the intensity of the memory as she walked toward the barn. She'd never seen such conflicting emotions, never known eyes could reveal so much. He'd been trying to deny it, but beneath the denial it was there. Heat, hunger, need. She'd felt it yesterday. She'd seen and felt it again today.

She understood those looks from men. The male of the species was rarely subtle. Why waste time on subtleties when a lie could net the same results? More than once she'd mistaken those lies for love.

She was past making those kinds of mistakes. There had been no love in Travis Dean's eyes. But in that moment he had desired her and he'd hated both himself and her because of it.

He was in Sissy's stall when she ducked into the barn and folded her arms over the top of the stall door. "She's gorgeous," she said softly and for a moment got lost in the miracle of birth.

The foal made her think of a wild fawn, all soft dun color and long, delicate legs. Currently, she was on her feet, rooting for her mom's milk, her little switch of a tail twitching like a flag in a flirty wind.

She shifted her gaze to Travis who was reloading the manger with hay. "Should be a good cross," he said, more to himself than to her.

"With Tucker?" she asked, referring to her father's foundation stallion. "Yeah. He's always crossed well on Sissy."

"Not this time. We bred her to my stud. Vi wanted to give it a go and see if we could come up with a buckskin."

At the mention of Vi's name, they both grew quiet.

Memories of the journal pages she'd decoded came tumbling back with crystal clarity. Should she tell him about them and about the message she'd found in the storm cellar? See what kind of reaction she got? She'd long ago dismissed concern about him having anything to do with Vi's death. And if the diaries were to be believed, they proved there was something much deeper, much more sinister that started long ago and followed Vi through the years.

And yet, she didn't tell him. It didn't feel right. It was all too surreal, too speculative at this point. She wanted to read more. She wanted to know more before she decided if what she was reading could possibly be fact, instead of wild fiction.

"You want to tell me the truth about the gun now?" he asked, dragging her back to the moment.

She was almost thankful for the reprieve. She didn't want to think about the diaries today. "I told you," she said and compounded the lie. She couldn't very well tell him she'd been spooked by what she'd read. She didn't like the feel of the lie, though, and wondered how it had been so easy for the men who had lied to her so many times. "I heard a coyote. At least I thought I did. I found the gun in the closet. Dad used to shoot at them to scare them off."

"Your dad, no doubt, knew how to use it. Do you?"

"You don't grow up on a ranch and not know how to handle a firearm." That, at least, was the truth.

His profile was hard, unreadable as he eased quietly beside the filly and scratched her lightly on the hip. It was a gentle touch, full of patience and intent to settle, to tame, to get her used to the touch of a man and to trust it.

He'd shown none of that patience with her. The thought crossed her mind like a bullet. Trust was an issue. He didn't trust her. Not on any level. She suddenly knew, in her heart, that it had been another woman who had made him that way.

"Clarence seems to think you're someone I can trust to do the right thing," she said straight-out because she wanted him to know it wasn't an issue for her. And because she was suddenly tired of waiting for his decision about the partnership. Her game plan of avoid and conquer be dammed.

His hand stilled momentarily before he went back to the process of gentling the foal. "Clarence is an old man."

"Who's a good judge of character." She worked to remain calm in the face of his cold comment.

He dropped his hand, looked at his boots, then looked at her. "I don't want to be your partner, Susannah."

She forced herself to hold his gaze. "So you've said. And I don't want to leave."

He compressed his lips, gave the filly one final scratch behind the ears and walked toward the door. She swung it open so he could exit the stall, then shut it in silence behind him.

"I don't understand why you don't just sell, take the money and run? Why do you want to make it so hard on yourself?" he asked as if he didn't have a clue what would possess her to want to stay here.

"You've got it wrong. I've been making it hard on myself for four years now. Staying is about changing all that. Staying is about what's right. For me. For the Rocking H. For my child," she said with as much strength and certainty as she could infuse in her voice.

He didn't seem to know how to respond. His gaze flicked to her rounding abdomen before he walked out of the barn and into the sunlight. She followed him, then stood by his driver's side door as he hiked himself up inside his truck and stared through the dusty windshield.

Hard eyes glanced at the swell of her abdomen again, then back to her face. "What about the father? Where does he fit into all of this?"

"If you're worried he's going to show up and try to stake a claim on me or the Rocking H, don't. He doesn't know I'm here."

His expression relayed a skepticism he didn't even try to conceal.

"He doesn't want to know," she added to make it clear that Jason was out of the picture. "He doesn't want anything to do with me or the baby."

Another long silence. Another long, searching look. Then he shoved in the clutch and turned the ignition.

What are you going to do, she wanted to demand. What's going to happen? But her better judgment kept her from giving in to the urge.

Let it be, she told herself. Let him think some more. Let him realize what he'd be doing to her if he refused to consider the partnership.

"I need to be here," she said and watched the muscle in his jaw bunch with what could have been anger or resolution or both. "My baby needs to grow up here." She resisted the urge to curl her fingers over his thick forearm where it rested on the open window frame and beseech him to consider what she'd just said. Instead, she stood back as he shifted into gear and hit the gas.

"You're damn good at leaving, aren't you?" she muttered to herself as she watched him pull away. It didn't surprise her. She was used to men driving away. And she was getting damn good at watching them go.

She checked her watch. She had a couple of hours before she had to shower and leave for her doctor's appointment. Even though she had wanted to avoid it, she couldn't stand it anymore. She walked back to the house and unlocked the file cabinet. Then she picked up the journals and once again began the laborious, but compelling work of decoding them.

Everyone in the know at Emory University—they were few as Henry insisted on absolute secrecy—were deliriously excited by Henry's research. He was, after all, world-renowned and to the moneymen at the university, Henry represented a cash cow. Early on, they increased funding for the project in anticipation of his success. They provided him with two young scientists, Dr. Agnes Payne, a fertility expert, and Dr. Oliver Grimble, a neurologist, to assist in the research. Oh, it was exciting! They named Henry's project Code Proteus—a title befitting a top-secret mission.

But, like all great work, success did not come overnight. From late 1963 through 1966, we labored tirelessly as a team, Oliver, Agnes, Henry and I....

Susannah scanned pages of details on the intricacies of the experimentation and research, then stopped and reread the next passage when she'd decoded it.

Finally, finally, we were on the cusp of the greatest experiment of all! It was time to bring all Henry's theories to fruition. It was time to implant genetically engineered human embryos into a surrogate female.

The anticipation was...I don't know how to describe it. Electric. Jubilant. And then the unexpected happened. The university cut off funding. Just like that. We were out of business. It seemed unbelievable that they would do such a thing now that we'd come so far, but because of Henry's insistence that the project remain top-secret, there had been no publicity to attract benefactors. No incoming contributions to defray the horrendous costs. Because everything was so expensive and it was taking longer than expected, the board—who didn't even know what the project entailed—shut us down.

It was over. All of our work. All of Henry's dreams. My heart broke for him. He was, of course, the most devastated of all. I'd seen him lost in the throes of grief. I'd seen him so focused on a task the rest of the world did not exist for him. I had never seen him angry.

It was cataclysmic the change that came over him. He was much like a wounded animal, ruled by pain. In an explosion of rage, he wrecked the lab while I could only stand by crying, frightened by this Jekyll and Hyde transition in him, destroyed by the loss of our dream.

Perhaps we should have taken the shutdown as an omen. If we had, Henry would be alive now. Henry would be alive and perhaps I wouldn't have had to give up my babies and live in hiding for the rest of my life to protect them....

"Susannah, this is a surprise." Del Brooks grinned up at her from behind a battle-scarred desk in his office at the Sheriff's Department. Colorful candy sprinkles trailed from an open box of chocolate-covered donuts and tracked over reams of coffee-stained reports to the paper napkin where a half-eaten donut rested at his elbow.

Still rattled over the journal entries she'd decoded just before she'd left for town, Susannah worked up a smile as Del set down a chipped coffee mug with faded red lettering advertising Al's Radiator Repair. He stood, wiping the back of his hand over a smear of chocolate at the corner of his mouth and extended his hand.

"I got your insurance papers last week and sent them right over to the agent."

"Oh, that's not why I'm here," she said, feeling edgy and uncertain suddenly.

The thing about working to avoid one problem was

that it left the mind free to address another. She didn't want to think about Travis's final decision regarding the partnership, so that led her back to Vi's journals. And that had led her to the note she'd found in the storm cellar. Not knowing for sure what she intended to do with it, she'd tucked it in her pocket just before she'd left for town. It wasn't until she'd pulled up in front of the County Sheriff's office after her OB checkup that she accepted she'd wanted to show it to Del. The note was all she was willing to share at this point. The journals were just too much of everything to share with anyone else just yet, if ever.

She glanced around the utilitarian office, noting the Salvation Army equipment, the coffeemaker in the corner about to burn dry and the dozens of wanted posters tacked to a yellowed bulletin board at his back.

"Want some coffee?" Del asked, already turning toward the pot. "Whoa," he turned back with a grimace. "Never mind. Bad idea this time of day. How 'bout a donut? Fresh this morning from the diner."

"No. I'm fine. Thanks."

She was more than nervous suddenly. Now that she was faced with actually revealing the original message...well, it all seemed a little out there.

"Something on your mind, Susannah?" Del asked, making her realize she'd been spending an inordinate amount of time studying the board full of posters she had absolutely no interest in reading.

She lowered her head, then turned to him. "I—I wanted to ask you...you're sure, without a doubt, that Vi's death was an accident, right? I mean you have ways...things you do to—I don't know—ways to measure speed and skid marks and angles and such to form a complete picture for you?''

Del sat back down in his chair, propped his elbows on his desk and steepled his fingers under his nose. ''You still fussing about that, honey?''

She looked away from the kindness in his eyes and the concern in his tone. ''I shouldn't be. I know. It's just, it's still hard to accept she would have lost control like that.'' She glanced back at his troubled scowl and pressed on. ''And the other person—what reason would they have had to be there? Doesn't it seem strange to you? I mean, it's not exactly a hotbed of tourism around here. Why would anyone but a local be driving that road?

''I don't suppose you've got an ID yet?'' she added when Del remained silent in the face of her questions.

''No, honey. We're still working on it.'' He paused, looking troubled. ''I wish there was something else I could say to make you feel better about this, but the fact is, accidents are harder to swallow sometimes than when something happens deliberately. That's why we call 'em accidents. It shouldn't have happened, no doubt about it. Vi shouldn't have died like that. But sadly, she did.''

He frowned, put on his fatherly lecture face. ''You need to ease up on yourself a bit, Susannah. Give it some more time.''

She understood why he was reluctant to go down that road. She really didn't want to go there, either, but she'd gotten this far. Reaching into her hip pocket, she tugged out the sheet of paper with the message and unfolded it.

''What's this?'' He glanced from her face to the note as she passed it over his desk.

She hugged her arms around herself, stared at the paper, instead of meeting his eye. "Just...um, just read it."

With furrowed brows, he looked from it to her again before he started reading. He was quiet for a long time, then tapped his thumb absently on his desk. "This Vi's handwriting?"

She shook her head. "It's mine. The original message—the one she left for me to find—was written in code."

She explained the notation she'd found in the computer and the subsequent coded message hidden in the storm cellar.

"I know," she said when his face folded into a knot of bafflement. "It's all very strange, but it makes more sense if you know that when I was little, Vi and I used to write notes to each other in code. It was like a game we played to pass snowbound or rainy days." She gestured toward the message. "For some reason, she felt a need to write this message in code."

"Where'd you say you found it, honey?"

She cleared her throat, trying to get a read on his thoughts. He'd recovered from the news of a coded message and schooled his face back into an unreadable scowl. If she were a betting woman, however, she'd guess he was leaning toward condescending patience for the loony who'd been away from the ranch for too long. "She'd hidden it in the storm cellar."

When he kept his gaze trained on the paper, she shook her head. "It sounds crazy, doesn't it? It probably is. I don't even know how long it was hidden there. Whether it was just last week, or—"

"Or maybe three or four years ago?" he prompted gently.

She nodded. "Yeah. I've thought of that." Again, she frowned, shook her head. "But something tells me it's more recent. Something tells me Vi was in some kind of trouble."

She watched as the sheriff slumped back in his chair, wrapped his lower lip around his upper and clearly struggled with what to say to her.

"You think I'm losing it, don't you?"

"No. Oh, no, honey. Nothing like that. I don't think that at all. It's just, well, it takes a pretty big leap of logic to turn Vi's death into foul play—and I take it that's the direction you're going with this?"

"Yes...maybe. I don't know. I don't know," she restated, feeling frustrated and confused and completely out of her league. She gestured toward the note. "But doesn't this make you wonder if maybe there was something going on?"

Again, he took his time, staring at the note, then lifting his gaze toward the tiny window that let some natural light into the room. When he spoke, his tone was infused with understanding. "My dad's got Alzheimer's. He'll be sixty-seven come December. He hid it from us kids and Mom for a long time. A long time," he repeated, and everything she knew of human nature told her he was silently berating himself for missing the clues, wishing there was something he could have done to see it or head it off or make that time easier for his father.

"Anyway." He flashed a sad smile, brought himself back to her and the moment. "He does and says strange things sometimes. Gets lost in the sixties, then lost altogether."

"You're saying you think Vi might have been delusional?"

He shook his head wearily. "No. Oh, hell, I don't know. I think I'm saying that things happen…to people we love, people we think we know. She was lonely, Susannah— Oh, no, now don't go lookin' like that, like someone just beat you black and blue. I'm not saying this to heap on more guilt when I can already see you're laying it on yourself with a dump truck.

"The thing is, we all got to do what we all got to do. You had your time. No one's blamin' you for it and you didn't cause anything to happen to Vi. But maybe this message was her way of connecting with the past and with you in some odd way. Maybe she was just passing some time, getting lost a little in her sorrow. What do you think?"

He'd risen and walked around the desk. He laid a comforting hand on her shoulder now.

"You're probably right," she said, wanting to believe his explanation more than she wanted to believe anything else. Wanting to discount the journals as the same thing.

"Been known to be," he said with an understanding smile. "Now you just quit worrying yourself over this. I'll be letting you know just as soon as we get an ID on the body, okay? You'll feel better when we get all the dust washed off that chapter of this book and we can give it complete closure."

"Yeah," she agreed and gave him the smile he wanted. "Listen, thanks for—"

"No thanks necessary. I'd a had the same concerns if I was in your shoes." He leaned back, snagged the note from the top of his desk and held it out to her. "I'd have had questions, too."

She folded the paper, tucked it back into her pocket. "Well, I'd better get moving."

"You doing okay out there by yourself?"

"I'm fine."

"Trav makin' sure everything's getting done?"

"Yeah," she said as he walked her toward the door. "He's making sure."

"Good man, Trav."

"So I keep hearing." She gave him another tight smile. I'm all right, see? it said. Not crazy. Not confused. Just a little…lost, she decided tiredly as she bid him goodbye and headed for her Blazer and the grocery store across town.

Nine

It was almost six by the time she turned into her lane. She'd picked up a few more groceries and filled the Blazer with gas before she'd headed home. She still had some money left from her small savings. She needed to make it last.

She had no idea how long it would be before the insurance payment came through. As always, the thought of Vi's life insurance gave her pause. It was both distressing and reassuring. She would use the money for the ranch. She'd already decided that. For expenses, for cash flow, for improvements. At least she would if she was still here when the insurance company sent the check.

Her heart did a little shuffle when she pulled up in front of the house and spotted Travis's pickup parked by the barn. His presence reminded her once again that whether she was still here when the check came hinged on his decision.

If it would have done her any good to get angry, she might have tried it. Anger, however, would be both misplaced and a waste of energy. The stone-faced Mr. Dean wasn't responsible for the terms of the will, just like he wasn't responsible for Vi's death.

If she'd had any lingering doubts, the testimony from his small army of supporters, led by Clarence and Del, and the entries she'd read so far from Vi's journal placed him well out of that loop. Every indication was that whatever Vi was afraid of had started many years ago back in Georgia.

Georgia. Not back east, as Vi had said whenever her past had come up. But south. Susannah was still having trouble digesting the information she'd decoded last night, as well as Del's conclusion about the original note. If he was right—and he very well could be—none of what she was reading was fact.

Still, she was itching to get back to the tedious work of decoding more pages to either prove or disprove Del's theory. That would have to wait now. Travis must have driven over for a reason.

She shouldered open the driver's side door and almost tripped over Sooner when she stepped out of the Blazer.

"Hey, girl," she bent over to scratch Sooner's ears. The collie showed more animation than Susannah had seen since she'd first arrived at the Rocking H. She was all wiggling hips, wagging tail and happy little yips. "Well, aren't you the happy dog?"

Her welcome compelled Susannah to go down on one knee and hug her. "Poor baby. Poor pretty girl. Did you think I wasn't coming back?"

"Appears that it crossed her mind," came a deep voice from behind her.

She looked up to see her neighbor walking toward her, Boomer charging out of the barn on his heels. When the little dog spotted her, he broke into a run and yapped his way to her side, quieting down only after she'd lavished him with praise and pats to the head.

"Crossed your mind, too, did it?" she asked, lifting

her gaze to Travis, unable to resist baiting him. "That I wouldn't come back?" she added.

"Well, sorry to disappoint you," she said when he merely glared. She was finished, she decided suddenly. She was finished walking on eggshells and dodging this confrontation. She needed an answer—even if it was the wrong one. "Sooner can rest easy. I don't plan on going anywhere. Unless I'm forced to," she added in defiance when she met the hard eyes shadowed beneath the brim of his Stetson.

He didn't bat a lash, didn't say a word as he jerked open the Blazer's tailgate and started unloading her groceries.

Susannah walked around to intercept him. She was irritated with herself for pushing him and with him for keeping her in this awful state of limbo. She understood why he was bucking the idea of a partnership, and couldn't even be annoyed with him for it. He had a life. He didn't need her as a complication. And how happy they'd both be if she didn't need him to complicate hers.

"You don't have to do that."

"You're right. I don't. And it's small comfort to know I still have some options, even if they are minor."

She went utterly still. Had she just heard something important? Eyes on his face, she walked to the lowered tailgate, waited for him to expand. Of course, he didn't. He walked toward the kitchen, his arms full of groceries.

She replayed his statement in her mind. Was that an "Uncle," she'd heard? Was that his cryptic way of saying he felt trapped by the partnership clause of Vi's will, but was resigned to it?

Anxious suddenly, she scrambled to catch up, then edged past him and up the porch steps and opened the door for him. "What did that mean, about options?"

Careful not to touch her, he strode past her into the kitchen and set the groceries on the counter. "It means, I don't like having my life manipulated—even by someone I considered my friend."

He turned and, propping his hands on his lean waist, met her eyes. "It means I'm not going to feed you to the wolves. I'm not going to let you lose the ranch or the profit you could realize from the sale of it."

Relief—hesitant, but hopeful—caught in her chest, rushed to her head.

"So," she said, struggling for calm when her heart wanted to leap out through her throat, "you're saying you're willing to agree to the partnership."

He stared at a spot on the wall above her head. "I'm saying I'll give you a year to make it work. Wait. Don't look so hopeful. If, at any time during that year, I'm not satisfied, if I see it's not working for either one of us, all bets are off. You either leave on your own, in which case the ranch gets sold and you get the money, or I'll terminate the partnership and you'll be left with a lot less cash."

To hide the trembling of her hands, she carefully dug into a sack and started pulling out milk and margarine and fruit that needed to go in the refrigerator. Elation. Hope. Relief. She knew it all showed in her face when she turned to him.

"Look, I know this isn't something you want to do. I'm sorry. I'm truly sorry you've been placed in this position. I'll do everything I can to hold up my end of the bargain.''

His smile was not kind. ''You're right. This isn't something I want to do. But I won't be the man to send a too-stubborn-for-her-own-good, single, pregnant woman out of her home.

''So, you win,'' he continued and stalked back toward the door. ''You've got your partnership, as short-lived as I expect it to be.''

''Wait.'' She shoved a gallon of milk into the fridge and hurried after him. ''What do you mean, short-lived? You said you'd give me a chance.''

He looked weary and put-upon. ''You'll get your chance. I don't expect to be the one to end this. You'll beat me to it.'' He thumbed back his Stetson. ''You're not going to last, Susannah. When you've had enough—whether it's next week or next month or even next spring—all you have to do is say so. It's going to be your decision, not mine.''

''And it really ticks you off, doesn't it?'' she asked, suddenly disgusted by his righteous, condescending and low opinion of her. ''I mean it big-time ticks you off that you've got a conscience and it's making you do something nice for me.''

He pushed out a snort. ''What I'm doing isn't nice. Don't mistake it for something that is.''

''Then what would you call it? Waylaying a guilty conscience?''

''Right now? Right now, I'd call it a mistake, but it's done. I won't go back on my word.''

''And I'll still be here next year.''

He gave her a long, hard look. ''I'll be back in the morning. We'll take a look at the books and you can get your bearings.''

And then, big surprise, he was gone. Again.

Your loss, she thought bitchily. "You could have had a free dinner," she told his dust trail. "And it would have been great!"

Trav popped the top on a beer and sank down in his recliner in front of the TV. He punched the remote until he landed on CNN and managed to keep his attention on the world news headlines for all of five minutes before he started thinking about the scene that had played out at the Rocking H a couple of hours ago.

Big blue eyes. That was what he saw, instead of the latest Middle East conflict. Defiant and hurt. He'd been a jerk. He'd known it and there hadn't been a damn thing he could do to stop himself.

And she'd been right—at least about one thing. He was *ticked,* as she'd so aptly put it. But it wasn't about his decision to give the partnership a go. That didn't settle, either, but he'd made his peace with it. No, it was something else eating at him.

It big-time ticks you off that you've got a conscience and it's making you do something nice for me. "Yeah, I was real nice all right," he grumbled as he slumped back in his recliner. "Prince of a guy. Charmed the pants right off of her."

Like hell. He hadn't charmed anything. But he wanted to—and that was what was getting to him.

Ever since he'd lifted her onto the back of his truck bed, ever since he'd seen her in her bed—hell, ever since he'd seen her hanging clothes in those short shorts and skimpy little top—he'd been as randy as a damn goat.

That was what he was ticked about.

To his utter disgust, despite their age difference and her pregnancy, despite every argument he'd concocted, he couldn't stop thinking about what it would be like to take her to bed. Susannah was the first woman—and there had been plenty since the divorce who had tried—to resurrect the libido Elena had all but killed with her infidelity.

He downed another swig of beer, settled in for some serious brooding. He'd enjoyed his life once. He suddenly found himself wanting to enjoy it again. Anger, he realized with a long, hard look at himself, took a lot of energy to maintain. And to what purpose? And why, he thought grimly, was it Susannah Hobson who had brought him to this conclusion?

He got up slowly when Boomer woofed, trotting back and forth between the living room and the kitchen, begging for his supper. Maybe because he'd come to grudgingly admire her determination and grit, he admitted as he dug into a bag of dry dog food and filled the schnauzer's bowl.

Leaning back against the kitchen counter, he stared out the window in the general direction of the Rocking H. Maybe because in spite of the mistakes she'd made, she was determined to go for the cards she wanted, instead of settling for the ones she'd been dealt.

So she'd made a mistake four years ago—and approximately five months ago, he added, thinking of the baby she carried. If he got pinned and pigeonholed by all the mistakes he'd made, well, the picture would be pretty grim. There was more to both of them than the sum total of their miscalculations. And she was right when she'd said he didn't know her. He still thought she'd duck and run when the going got tough, though, but he was determined to give her a little room, let her at least try. She deserved that much from him.

And what do you deserve from her, boyo?

Nothing. He tossed his beer bottle in the recycle bin. Not one damn thing.

Susannah was ready for her "partner" the next morning. She was tired of his cat-and-mouse games. Buoyed by his decision to give the partnership a go, she'd risen early and watched for his truck. If this was truly going to work, he was going to have to get used to dealing with her. He'd no more than pulled into the drive and she rushed outside and invited him in for breakfast. He'd been too surprised by her sneak attack to think of an excuse to turn her down.

"Right now I'm limited as to what I can contribute," she explained, referring to her pregnancy as they sat at the table, while Sooner and Boomer nosed around outside. "Until I can work alongside you, I'll try to make it up in other ways. Feeding you will be one of them."

His usual stoicism had stalked into the kitchen with him. But when he sat down to Denver omelets, golden hash browns, hot rhubarb muffins and strong coffee, she sensed a small lifting of his guard.

"One of my many jobs during the past four years," she said as he dug in, "was as a short-order cook."

He angled her a considering look.

"Not too glamorous, but it paid the rent and kept me fed. Plus I learned how to cook."

"That you did," he agreed with the most enthusiasm she'd heard since she'd met him. "What else have you done?"

She shrugged, encouraged because he'd initiated a question that didn't start or end with dialogue on why she should reconsider her decision to stay. "A little bit of everything. Left a cushy position tending bar to come home," she said with a grin. "It didn't take long to figure out that without some kind of a degree, the jobs would be limited and the pay minimal. So I worked and took classes and worked and took classes." She poured him more coffee.

"Classes in what?"

"Office administration. Bookkeeping. Computers. Anything that might help me get a position where I'd find a little job security and manage on more than a shoestring budget. I'd have finished up this fall if…well, if things had turned out differently," she finally said.

His gaze dropped to her abdomen. A baby changed things. Changed plans. Changed priorities.

He became very quiet then. So did she. That had been two hours ago and since then, except for the occasional comments on her cooking, the weather and Sooner's impending delivery, which should be anytime now, neither had much else to say.

But it was a different kind of silence than she was used to around him, she told herself as she'd braved his scowl and followed him through chores, which he'd insisted on doing since he was here. If not a comfortable silence, at least the hostility was lacking.

Now it was close to noon. They'd been planted in front of the computer for over an hour. He'd been showing her the books, explaining the spreadsheets, acting like he had expectations of her. Susannah was happy. She wanted to play an active part in the partnership and this was one area she could make a contribution.

"After your dad died," he said when they ran across a notation to renew one of the grazing permits, "Vi continued to work with the Forest Service on a rotational grazing system for the cattle. I think she told me once that Dale got his first permit back in the sixties.

"Anyway, the system had been modified over the years, but Vi had been pretty proud the land showed the benefits of Dale's stewardship. She actually started giving tours last fall to promote the benefits of holistic range management."

"You're kidding."

"It seemed to be something she really enjoyed. She explained about grazing management practices—rotation, fire and weed control—and how it all enhances range health, wildlife habitat and water quality."

"Sounds like you're invested in it, too." The tenor of his voice made it clear he agreed with Vi's methods.

"It only makes sense."

And it was beginning to feel like it made sense they were here, working together. At least it felt like it to her. He was sincere, informed and cognizant of what it was going to take to keep the operation in the black.

"I've been trying to figure out this entry."

He leaned forward to get a better look at the screen, accidentally brushing her shoulder in the process. At the slight contact, he pulled back as if he'd been burned. She'd certainly felt the heat of the unexpected touch, felt it in the form of a sizzling awareness.

She looked over her shoulder to see if he'd felt it, too. His gaze was locked on the screen, but the heavy surge of his pulse at the base of his throat gave him away. Yeah. He'd been affected.

"It's a record of the alfalfa and hay supply," he said, his voice tight. "She had a good crop last year."

"Unless there was a winter drought, we've always gotten a good crop." She peeled her gaze away from the tanned skin at his throat and looked at the monitor. "Dad always said it was the altitude. Makes for high-quality hay regardless of the short growing season. Am I reading this right? There was extra last year Vi didn't need for the cattle?"

"Yeah, this entry shows what she got for it when she sold the excess."

He was so close she could see the dark cobalt flecks in the startling blue of his eyes. She could see the heaviness of the beard he'd shaved close this morning. She could smell his aftershave, a dizzying mix of musk and leather and something that made her think of mountain sage and midnight shadows.

He was feeling the awareness, too. Mixed with the sensual heat was a grudging appreciation of her knowledge.

"We always did count on it for an extra source of revenue."

He appeared surprised that she was aware of that fact.

"I know what it takes to run this ranch," she said, because he needed to be reminded of it as much as to ease the awareness of their closeness. "The horse herd was trailed to the winter pasture in December, right? If I remember, that's the meadow closest to the house."

"Yeah." His voice sounded gruff. "We needed

easy access to that part of the herd. We fed them there until April."

"Is the other part of the herd still pastured year-round on BLM land?"

He nodded. "It's where most of the calves dropped."

"And let's see... By that time, the yearlings had already been delivered to the north pasture, branded and vaccinated, and the horses trailed back home by the end of the month. We still have BLM in on that mix, too?"

Again, he nodded. "Payments are registered in this column. They're due next week by the way."

She dragged her attention away from his face, too aware of yet more contrasts—his granite-hard jaw, the softness of his lips, the clean, crisp lines of his high cheekbones, the butterfly softness of his thick blond lashes. She made herself study the spreadsheet. "Are these expenses telling me the meadows were dragged and fertilized in May?"

"Right." He pointed with his index finger, careful not to touch her again. "And this is the irrigation fee for the month."

"Last month you would have branded and vaccinated the spring calves, rounded up the yearling cattle and trucked and trailed them into the Forest allotments, right? So what's up next?"

"The second crop of hay is mowed and dry and ready to put up. I'd like to get it in before it rains, but from the looks of the sky when I came in, that's not going to happen."

"You need help," she said.

"I told you I could handle it."

Stubborn. It showed in more than the set of his jaw.

And full of pride. Her dad had been like that. He'd worked from dawn to dusk every day of his life. He'd never complained. He'd loved what he'd done. He'd also died way too young from working too hard.

The magnitude of work that lay ahead for Travis the rest of the year was daunting. She was due to deliver in late November. In early October when the cattle needed to be gathered in preparation for shipping mid-month, she'd be big as a blimp. When the calves were weaned and pregnancy checks made on the herd, the baby would be here and need her complete attention. Not until late December would she be able to start pulling her weight, assuming she could find a sitter. And until then, he still had to contend with all of the other year-round operations such as building and repairing fence, repairing machinery and breaking horses.

Whether he liked it or not, they needed some extra hands, at least temporarily. And the next time he showed up, they were going to have them. Rachael had called again yesterday and she'd made up her mind. She was going to hire the Scott boys. She could handle them.

"Look, I've got to be heading out," he said abruptly and stood. "If the storm front that's supposed to move in tonight is as strong as they're forecasting, I need to move a little stock around."

She felt herself redden when she realized she'd been staring at the face that suddenly fascinated her. Felt more the absence of all his male strength and heat at her back.

"Lunch," she said, thrashing about for something to distance herself from the unexpectedly sensual moments hovering between them. "Let me at least feed you."

He shook his head. "I really need to get going." He was already reaching for the door. "Watch the sky, okay? I'll be back tonight to batten things down. Earlier if I can make it. I turned Sis and the filly out this morning, but I'll need to round them back up if the weather turns bad."

Just that fast, he was gone. And she was left wondering what had happened.

"What do you think, baby-baby?" she murmured, rubbing her palm in a soothing caress over her belly where the baby kicked or turned or stretched and made her smile. "Is he running scared?"

Where that notion came from, she didn't know. But it settled and formed into something more than speculation as she walked into the kitchen and poured herself a glass of milk. For days, he'd been nothing but hasty retreats, brooding silences and hard, cold glares. Obviously, he'd made peace with his lot in her life—or, more to the point, with her lot in his. More and more, she suspected Clarence was right. Travis Dean was a good man. He hadn't been able to turn her out; he'd swallowed his pride and was treating her like a true partner.

And a bit like a leper, she thought with a frown. The man did not want to touch her, or he was determined not to touch her. One of the two. She suspected it was the latter.

The sexual awareness she'd sensed since that first morning when he'd shown up on his horse was still simmering like water on low boil. But where once it had been tempered by his anger, now there was something else in the mix. Their working relationship had changed the dynamics on several counts. Without his anger to hide behind, it seemed the brooding Mr. Dean didn't know how to mask what he was feeling for her.

And exactly what was he feeling, she wondered as she made herself a sandwich then happily fed half of it to Sooner who woofed it down like it was the best thing she'd ever eaten.

"And what exactly are *you* feeling, Susannah Lyn?"

She wasn't oblivious to the way he watched her. And she wasn't oblivious to her own reaction to him. He was darkly attractive. The chemistry had been there from the beginning. She'd been wondering for some time now whether it was pain, not indifference, he hid behind his dark scowls. He'd had a past before he came to Colorado, and, even though Clarence hadn't seen fit to share it with her, that past was shadowed with something that made him the way he was. Brooding. Guarded. Lonely.

Yeah, she decided as she ran fresh water in Sooner's bowl. The man was lonely. It was easy to recognize the signs when you knew the meaning of the word up close and personal. It takes a lonely soul to know one. But did she really want to know Travis Dean?

Well, it didn't matter, she thought, munching on a crisp apple. It didn't matter that she was drawn to him or that he was drawn to her. She wouldn't act on it. In fact, she was just as determined as he was to keep their relationship—whatever that relationship was—from evolving into something physical.

But knowing, even recognizing the sexual awareness, didn't make it any less puzzling. It didn't help that she wasn't entirely clear about why he'd decided to give the partnership a try. Most men she'd known hadn't offered to do anything for her unless they'd had very clear ulterior motives. He didn't appear to have any motives except helping her. Could he actually be the physical embodiment of the age-old myth of the last good man, she thought with a derisive grin.

She'd have given it more thought, but when she walked toward her bedroom with the notion of taking a quick nap, she had to pass by the den. She stopped in the doorway. Hesitated. Stared for a long time at the file cabinet where she'd locked Vi's journals and her transcribed notes.

Without thinking, she raised her hand to what was becoming the familiar weight of the rings hanging around her neck. The small file cabinet key hung on the chain now, too. It felt benign yet somehow dangerous. What secrets would it unlock?

She wished she could just let it go. But the truth was, she still wasn't convinced Del was right. The next thing she knew, she was kneeling before the cabinet and inserting the key in the lock. A distant rumble of thunder had her looking out the window.

The sky was overcast, but not threatening. Gray clouds hung low and still over the mountain range. The breeze lifting the curtains was gentle, cool and carried the distinctive scent of ozone.

She saw that Sissy and her baby had wandered up to the barn so she decided to take advantage of the circumstances and tuck them into their stall. She found a lead rope in the barn, hooked it on Sis's halter and with the foal stuck to her momma's side like a burr, resettled them.

The first fat raindrop fell just as she hit the back porch. She was already thinking past the rain to the journals. After pouring a glass of tea, she turned the kitchen radio on low then walked into the living room. Curled up on the sofa with Vi's pages in her lap and a pen in her hand, she fell headlong into the unfolding drama.

Henry gathered his composure after he wrecked the lab. And we tried everything we could think of to convince the university to reinstate funding. But they remained firm. They remained rigid. It was then that we found out money was not the only issue. Some of the studies on genetic engineering Henry had allowed to be published had created heated debate in academic circles. Ethical and philosophical questions had arisen and the university suddenly regarded his work as too risky. Little did we know how right they were.

Still, when all looked lost, Henry regrouped. He knew that a scientific research wing of the CIA called Medusa had been observing his research from afar. He knew, because he'd been approached by a man named Willard Croft, a former Harvard scientist and fellow genetics expert, to join Medusa. One phone call was all it took—and miracles began to happen.

Within a matter of weeks, Code Proteus was funded again and arrangements were made to move the project to Belle Terre where Henry could carry on his research without fear of exposure to the outside world and without risk of budget cuts.

I rolled up my sleeves and dug in, doing everything I could to assist Henry and Oliver and Agnes to pack—only to be advised that I would not be making the transition with them.

I'd been deluding myself, it seems, into believing I

was truly a part of the team. I can't begin to describe my disappointment when they left me behind. Not only would I lose contact with the most exciting scientific research of our time, but I would lose contact with Henry. Both had become my life.

I realized then that when I was nineteen, what I had felt for Henry had truly been infatuation. But I'd worked beside him for three years now and infatuation had grown to love. Lasting and true. I love him still. I miss him still.

But I'm letting myself drift off again and what I record next requires clarity of thought.

So, there I was, bereft, but stoically accepting I would not be going with the three scientists to Belle Terre, when at the eleventh hour I was invited to join them. I didn't even question why. I was so afraid they'd change their mind. It wasn't until years later that Henry revealed the reason for my inclusion. It seemed Medusa had concerns that I knew too much and represented a potential security risk, that I might even sell my knowledge of Code Proteus to Russia or China out of spite for being left behind. Henry, of course, had known the idea was preposterous. Medusa, however, had remained firm and insisted that if I wasn't included in the research I would have to be silenced in some effective manner. It was at that precise moment Henry became concerned that he may have made a deal with the devil.

I was unaware of any of this at the time. What I was made aware of was that there were conditions attached to my inclusion. If I wished to continue as a part of the team, I was to serve as surrogate mother to the genetically enhanced embryos.

Ten

Susannah stopped, reread the passage to make sure she'd unscrambled it correctly. Then she let out a deep breath and stared into space. She didn't begin to know how to digest this. Vi was to give birth to genetically enhanced children?

Cognizant suddenly that the rain was coming down in steady, heavy sheets, Susannah checked all the windows. She returned to the sofa, stared at the pages for several long seconds, then finally sat back down. She had to know. She had to know what happened next.

I loved Belle Terre. I thrived there at the North Carolina oceanfront estate just outside the sleepy little seaside village. I nested in the old antebellum mansion that was off the beaten path as the cool breezes and slow moving fans stirred air rich with the scent of spring and flowers and growth.

They'd thought it was a sacrifice on my part, agreeing to carry and give birth to the babies, but it had been my secret dream, especially since I'd known all along Henry would be the sperm donor. I was so in love with him, blinded by it, that I overlooked the bizarre circumstances and actually fantasized about carrying his children. The only disappointment we suffered during that first critical month was that of the five implanted eggs, only three attached.

But the three—what a thrill to know they were developing normally. I was, as any expectant mother is, proud, anxious, protective.

And Henry, it seemed, was also affected as he watched my pregnancy progress. I could see the hunger growing in his eyes—hunger for the wife and children he'd lost. I was determined to do everything in my power to ensure these babies flourished inside me and grew healthy and strong for him....

Susannah scanned several decoded pages, then skipped ahead to see what happened next.

It's true what they say about the birth process. Even though Henry and I had not conceived these children in the traditional way of mutual love and physical unity, it felt as if we had when the time came for me to deliver under the expert attention of Henry and Agnes and Oliver right there at the mansion where we had constructed a state-of-the-art delivery room.

My babies—and they were my babies, no matter that this had started as a scientific experiment—were so beautiful. My heart wept with love for my baby girl and my two little boys. But soon, I was to weep with grief. I'd known before they'd told me that something was wrong.

"Where are you taking him?" I cried as Agnes carried the painfully still bundle from the room. "Where is she taking him?" I demanded of Oliver. When he hung his head and looked away, I appealed to Henry. He took my hand, held it in his. "He's in a better place now," he said as a tear trailed down his cheek.

My baby boy—an angel. And I'd never seen his face.

Love for little Grace and Jake pulled me through.

I never forgot, but the pain dimmed and I vowed my grieving would not affect them in any way....

Lightning cracked in a jagged, angry arc across the darkening sky. Susannah flinched involuntarily then winced again when a booming blast of thunder followed on its heels. Her body tingled with residual energy from the storm that was now gathering in earnest over the mountains. Her mind swam with the lingering implication of the last of the words she'd decoded.

Babies. Had they actually created genetically altered babies? She shut out the sound of the rain pelting the windows like bullets from the west now as the wind picked up, shuttling the front through the valley.

What had they done? And how much deeper into this did she really want to go? If the journals were factual accounts of Vi's life, was she placing herself in danger with every discovery she made? And if so, could she afford to continue? Could she afford *not* to?

Another sharp report of thunder brought her head up. She was surprised to see how dark the afternoon had become while she'd been engrossed decoding the journals. On its heels, a teeth-rattling explosion jarred her off the sofa and her mind out of the diary that had sucked her in like a funnel cloud, siphoning up everything in its path.

In the background the static beep from the radio alerted her to a weather warning.

"This is a first alert forecast from your 98.6 weather team. The National Weather Service out of Denver has issued a severe thunderstorm warning for portions of our listening area. A band of fast-moving storms with the potential of heavy rains and damaging winds has been picked up by Doppler radar. The cell is currently moving to the east, southeast at twenty to thirty miles an hour through the Jackson County valley south of Walden. Persons in the path of this storm are advised to take cover immediately. Repeat. The National Weather Service..."

A little disoriented by the storm, by the utter scope and drama of the journals, Susannah felt emotionally spent suddenly, unable to continue until she could digest the import of the information. No wonder Vi had hidden the diaries. No wonder she'd written them in code. There was danger here. And now Susannah must protect the information as Vi had.

Thunder continued to roll and lightning crackle around her as she climbed the stairs to the attic, grabbing a flashlight on the way in case the electricity went out. She was in the process of hiding the diaries and her pages of deciphered notes back in the secret compartment beneath the bottom attic step when the lights flickered, dimmed then went black. Simultaneously, a loud bang startled a strangled scream out of her.

Pressing a hand to her heart, she calmed herself with assurances that the wind, which had picked up in the past hour, had probably slammed something against the house. Flicking on the flashlight, she walked cautiously downstairs.

The day had turned dead-of-night black. Rain drummed the windows like bullets, firing like spent shells against the house in sideways sheets.

"It's okay, girl," she assured Sooner who had tucked her tail between her legs and ducked her head. She searched a kitchen drawer for matches to light the hurricane lamp and lifted it down from the top of the refrigerator. "We'll be fine. This house has stood for—" She bit her last words off on a gasp when the back door flew open and crashed against the wall.

Rain lashed through the opening, drenching the kitchen floor and the dark silhouette of the man filling the open doorway. Terror sliced through her in icy shards, then receded on a trembling breath when she recognized him.

"Travis! My God." She clutched the counter for support. "You scared me to death. What in the world are you—" She stopped short when he sagged against the wall. "Oh, God." She rushed to his side. "You're hurt."

He grunted, attempted to push her back. "Get away. I'm soaked. Muddy." He reached back for the door, tried to close it, but apparently didn't have the strength.

"Stay right there," she demanded. Propping him against the wall, she stepped around him, wrestled the door shut and turned back to look him over.

He was drenched to the bone in rain and mud and... Oh, Lord. Blood. It poured into his eyes, trailed down his cheek, spread like a stain down his neck and darkened the collar and shoulder of his drenched chambray shirt to a rusty black.

"What happened?" She lifted his arm and draped it over her shoulder then tried to help him to a kitchen chair.

"Don't—"

"Shut up! Just lean on me. Let me get you down in a chair before you fall down."

"Boomer." He turned back toward the door, grimaced in pain when he tried to put weight on his left leg. He swore, and caught himself with a hand on the counter and kept himself from going down.

"He's out there?" she managed, reaching for a chair and dragging it to him since she couldn't get him to the chair. She pushed him down, then ran back and swung open the door.

"Boomer!" The blast of rain hit her face and soaked her blouse. "Boomer! Come!"

The little schnauzer scrambled up the porch steps like a drowned rat. He made a beeline into the kitchen, skittering between her feet on his way by. He shook himself violently. Water and mud sprayed all over the kitchen. Then he stood there shivering, while Susannah wrestled the door closed again.

She'd deal with the frightened dogs and the mess later. Pushing her sodden hair back from her face, she grabbed the dish towel hanging from the refrigerator door handle.

"I need to stop the bleeding," she said, moving in front of him.

He grabbed the towel and pressed it to his forehead. "It's not as bad as it looks."

"Yeah, well, if it's only half as bad, you need a doctor."

"It's a head wound. They bleed. It's nothing."

"Not from where I'm standing. Now quit being so darn belligerent and macho and whatever else you think you need to be and just let me look at it."

The last came out on a shout. Fear did that to a person. Adrenaline spiked. Nerves frayed. She wrestled them back. Calmly shoving his hand aside, she lifted the blood-soaked towel away from his head and inspected the damage.

"God." She swallowed back the slick swell of nausea. "What hit you?"

He grunted, winced, as she dabbed the towel to a jagged gash just inside his hairline above his forehead. It wasn't that it was deep. It was the swelling going on underneath that created the bleeding.

"Felt like a tank."

Some of her tension eased out on a ragged breath. She managed a small smile, as he'd intended. "Yeah, well, since the nearest tank battalion is a couple of states away, try again. Hold this. Yes, right there. Not so much pressure. I'll get something to clean it."

She hurried to the downstairs bathroom and dug around in the cabinet for cotton balls, peroxide, clean washcloths and towels. When she returned to the kitchen, he'd slid down in the wooden chair, his butt propped on the very edge, his shoulders pushing into the chair back. His left leg was extended straight out in front of him, his mouth twisted in pain.

"What? What else is hurt?" she demanded, rushing to his side.

"My ankle," he ground out and sucked in a breath, straining with the effort to keep from wincing. "Twisted it bad. Got to get the boot off...while I still can."

With a firm hand on his shoulder, she eased him back when he tried to lean forward and pull it off. "You're going to make it worse."

They both knew she was right. And they both knew what had to be done.

"Tell me if I hurt you."

He pushed out a humorless laugh that pretty much told the tale. There was no way she could avoid hurting him. "Just do it."

She turned her back to him, straddled his leg and gripped the heel of his boot with both hands. Way too aware of how agonizingly painful this was for him, she carefully lifted, got a good grip and pulled.

"Do it," he ground out when she hesitated, reacting to the groan he couldn't quite manage to bite back.

"I can't get it. The leather's too wet, so is your sock. Your ankle's too swollen already." Very carefully, she lowered his foot to the floor again. She stepped over his leg and without debating, walked to the cupboard drawer where the household tools were kept.

When she turned back to him, she was wielding a set of leather cutters. He looked from it to her face and shook his head in resignation. And then he actually whined.

"Gawddamm. They're my favorite boots."

She just stared at him. He was bleeding, in acute pain, and the first sign of weakness he showed was over the loss of a piece of leather.

She dropped to her knees in front of him. "Knowing that is going to make this a whole lot more fun for me."

She looked up at him then. And in spite of the blood, the mud and the pain, when their eyes met in the storm-darkened kitchen, they both smiled.

An hour later, his left boot was a memory. He was also stripped to the skin, relatively dry and lying on the sofa wrapped in an old quilt. His head was clean and bandaged; his foot was propped up on the arm of the living room sofa, cushioned with pillows and packed in ice. He was also in less pain, thanks to the aspirin she'd insisted he take or else.

Yeah. His boot was a memory. He had a whole slew of other memories to keep him company as he drifted to the sound of the wind and rain and his thoughts strayed back to the kitchen where she was still working to clean up the mess.

"Nurse Ratchet has nothin' on me," she'd said as she bandaged him, then bundled him from head to toe in a quilt. Her smile was ornery, no doubt to cover the fact that she was worried about him. She'd wheeled the desk chair from the den into the kitchen, helped him into it then wheeled him into the living room and settled him on the sofa.

All of this was accomplished with cool, composed efficiency. She'd been as professional as an EMT, as reserved as a stranger—if you didn't count the nervous little glances she'd flicked his way from beneath the thick fringe of her lashes. If you discounted the ultra sensitive touches from her cool steady hands.

Outside, the storm crashed and raided and growled with the rage of a wounded bear. Inside, she'd lit an oil lamp and half-a-dozen candles. The soft light had flickered and swayed across her face as she'd tended to his wounds.

Awareness. It had hummed in the dimly lit kitchen. Another man might have been able to ignore it. Another man might have wanted to.

She'd been an oasis of calm in a storm of pain. His ankle had throbbed like a bitch. Still did, but it was easing. She'd seen to that. Just as she'd seen to unbuttoning his shirt, peeling the soaked chambray off his shoulders, pulling it free of his jeans. He'd drawn the line when she'd reached for his belt buckle. Not from any surge of strength on his part. But from weakness. If she'd touched him there, he'd have folded.

Pain or no pain, blood or no blood, he'd have finally tasted those full lips that had been haunting him for too many nights to count.

"Christ," he muttered and threw his arm over his eyes. He was hopeless.

"What's wrong?"

He lifted his arm to see her hurry into the living room from the kitchen.

Everything, he thought. Everything was wrong. Except the look on her face.

Was he so pathetic now? Had he descended so far that the thought of a woman caring about him, worrying about what happened to him, fussing over his comfort, could reduce him to wanting to be someone who mattered?

"Is it your ankle?" she asked anxiously, oblivious to the emotions roiling inside him.

She carefully lifted the quilt up and off of his foot, then checked the ice pack, winced when she saw the extent of the swelling. "Maybe we need to take the ice off for a while. I know there's a pressure wrap around here somewhere. Maybe—"

"It's all right," he said gruffly. "I'm all right. Quit worrying about me and get yourself into some dry clothes."

Please, he added silently. Her shirt was still wet from the rain, from contact with him. The fabric was thin. It left little to the imagination. And as his gaze dropped to her breasts, lingered, he became aware that she was having her own trouble with all this forced intimacy.

Her nipples hardened into tight little peaks, pressing against the wet blouse under which the delicate lace design of her bra was clearly defined.

"I, um, I've just about got the mess cleaned up in—in the kitchen," she stammered. "Then I'll—I'll just, um, change."

She backed up a step, spun around, and left the room. Trav let his head fall back, stared at the ceiling. He ran the heel of his hand along the ridge of his erection and prayed for the rain to stop.

And then, unbelievably, he slept.

Susannah hated to wake him because he'd been in so much pain, but it had been an hour since she'd found him like this, dead to the world. He was deeply asleep. At the look of him, a word came to mind she would have never before associated with Travis Dean. Vulnerable.

He looked utterly vulnerable as he lay there, his big body crowded on the faded floral sofa. His head was turned to the side on the pillow, his thick lashes kissing the crest of his cheeks. His face didn't look hard now. In the pale candlelight, it looked almost poetic. His full lips were relaxed, instead of compressed in the thin, tight line that was a perpetual part of his scowl. His hair had dried. It curled softly at his ear, spilled over the white bandage she'd wrapped around his head with gauze to hold it in place.

He must have gotten warm as he lay there. Even though the rain pummeled and the wind swatted at the windows like a hungry tiger, it was still July. An unnatural warmth, heavy with humidity and thick with ozone, filled the air. He'd pushed the quilt down almost to his waist.

She felt herself blush as she watched the steady rise and fall of his broad chest. She knew what it felt like to touch the light dusting of pale, golden hair covering it. When she'd helped him out of his wet shirt, her fingers had brushed across the rise of hard pectoral muscle, grazed the breadth of his deeply tanned back.

His skin had been cold to the touch then. As cold as it was warm now.

Vulnerable. Yes, it was a word she would never have linked with him before. As she looked at him now, another word came to mind she had no business placing anywhere near him. *Lover.*

She couldn't help but wonder. What would it be like to be touched by him? What would it be like to be loved by him—by this man, not some boy who played at being one.

He was toned and lean and firm all over. It had been impossible not to notice. He was over six feet tall, must weigh in at around one-ninety. A man that size—naked, but for the tuck and twist of an ancient quilt—filled up a fair share of her living room. Took up the lion's share of the sofa. And crowded her thoughts with ideas way too vivid for her own good.

"Travis," she said gently. "Travis, you need to wake up."

He opened his eyes slowly, winced when he moved his leg. "What? What's wrong?"

"Nothing. It's... You might have a concussion. You shouldn't sleep too much if that's the case."

He blinked off the lingering effects of sleep, closed his eyes again and shifted, trying to get more comfortable. "What time is it?"

"Almost six. I made soup. Good thing the range is gas."

"Soup?" He grunted, scrubbed a hand over his face. "It's got to be eighty degrees in here."

"Yeah, well, sue me. It's the standard cure for everything. Do you feel like sitting up?"

In answer, he wedged himself to a sitting position and gingerly propped his foot on the footstool she'd placed by the sofa. "You're making way too much of this."

"Well, since the storm doesn't show any sign of letting up and that makes you more or less a captive audience, I guess you'll just have to put up with it. How *is* the ankle?"

"Better than my boot. Which you enjoyed ruining way too much, by the way."

"We take our pleasures when we can."

His gaze singed her with a look so hot, she felt the burn to her toes. "Um…I'll just get you some crackers."

Setting the bowl of soup on the TV tray she'd found in the closet, she hightailed it out of the room and into the kitchen. There she stood, pressing her palms to her cheeks.

This was not good.

She dug in the cupboard for the crackers, poured some in a basket then fixed them both a glass of iced tea. When she headed back into the living room, she was in control again—until she saw the slipping quilt. It was one thing to watch him as he slept. It was another to see him sitting up, all those chest and bicep muscles flexing as he braced his hands on either side of his hips to lever himself into a more comfortable position.

And it was quite another to see the pale line of his bare hip, the muscled swell of his thigh.

"I, um…"

He looked from her wide eyes to his lap where the quilt was about to take a major southward dive. He snatched it up and covered himself, then stared dead ahead at the wall.

"Why don't I go see if I can find, um, something for you to wear until…well, until your clothes dry."

Clutching the quilt in his fist, he slumped back against the sofa cushions. "Yeah," he said, his voice wooden. "Why don't you do that."

It was only sheer dumb luck that she had a pair of sweats to fit him. She'd bought the men's size large gray sweat pants on sale at a discount store on impulse one day while she was still in Wyoming. The baggy pants and drawstring waist had seemed just the ticket to accommodate her expanding waistline. And the price had been right.

She wasn't sure how he'd managed to get them on and wasn't about to ask as she cleared up his empty soup bowl and refilled his glass of tea. Drip-dried and glad to be out of the rain, Boomer had curled up on the area rug in front of the TV. Sooner, uncomfortable with storms, had willingly ducked into the hall closet and made a little nest of the old blanket Susannah had tossed on the floor for her.

The electricity was still out. So were the phones. There was nothing to do but wait it out. And try to ignore the storm of awareness that continued to build inside her.

"You're still bleeding a little," she said when she noticed the telltale seepage of red through the gauze bandage. "Maybe I'd better take a look at it."

His hand lashed out and snagged her wrist before

she could touch him. "Leave it. It's fine. Thanks anyway," he added taking some of the bite out of his clipped rebuff.

"So," she said after a long moment in which she'd worked to regain the equilibrium he'd thrown off kilter with his harsh words and surprisingly gentle grip on her wrist. She brushed the fingers of her other hand across the places where he'd touched her. Her skin still burned there.

Sitting down across from him in an overstuffed chair, she tucked her feet up under her bottom. "You never did say what happened."

He lifted his glass, draining a good portion of it before he set it down. He waited a bit longer before he decided he was going to share. "I'd battened down at home and driven over to make sure you were okay," he said after a while. "I'd just pulled up in your drive when all hell broke loose. It'd been bad for the past hour or so, but by that time the wind was blowing the rain against my truck so hard it was rocking. I couldn't see through my windshield."

As if to emphasize his statement, lightning flared like a strobe; thunder exploded in its wake.

"I'd just ducked out of my truck and was heading for the house when I heard this deafening crack. I looked up just in time to see half a tree looking for a place to land."

"The big cottonwood?"

"'Fraid so."

"No wonder you've got a lump on your head the size of an egg."

He lifted a hand to his head, gingerly explored with his fingers.

"Okay," she amended when he arched a brow.

"So I exaggerated a little. It looked that big when your blood was gushing out of it."

"Yeah, well, it's minor."

"Compared to your ankle."

"Yeah. Compared to that. I must have twisted it when I went down."

"I found the compression wrap." She nodded toward the end table where she'd placed it in easy reach for him.

She let him struggle with the wrap for a while. The grim set of his mouth made it clear that despite the pain, he was too stubborn to ask for her help. When she couldn't stand it any longer, she got up and without a word knelt in front of him.

His ankle had to be killing him. He had yet to utter a word of complaint. It softened her heart toward him. Toward this stoic man who so did not want to let his feelings show.

And that was what Travis Dean was all about. He didn't want to let anyone into his thoughts, to his hopes, to his dreams. To his fears. He had them all. She was sure of it. What she wasn't sure of was what made him so afraid of showing anyone those parts of himself.

She handled his ankle carefully. When she was done, she sat back on her heels and looked up into his eyes. What she saw stunned her. Made her want to weep.

Longing—more than sexual, deeper than need— burned in the glittering blue eyes she'd always thought of as cold.

She saw them clearly now that his shields were down. They weren't cold. They were haunted. And right now they hungered for something that went beyond the physical.

She rose to her knees, aware that if she hadn't done it on her own power, he would have lifted her. He'd already reached for her, already touched his big, scarred hands to her shoulders, caressed her, pulled her unerringly toward him.

She couldn't look away from him, from the way his gaze tracked across her face as if he was searching for answers even as he denied the existence of questions. And yet they were undeniable. Can I trust this? Can I trust you?

The strained tension that always surrounded them shifted by degrees to balance on yet another knife-sharp edge, as fierce as the storm and just as powerful.

Suddenly it was easy to let down her guard. To feel cocooned in the candlelight, suspended in the absolute rightness of the moment. It was essential to let emotions sway at the urge of impulse and answer the need in his touch.

His eyes met hers one final time. One final plea. She nodded, touched her fingers to his cheek. Trust me. Kiss me. Hold me.

When he lowered his head to hers, she met him halfway, sinking into his kiss like a slow-falling sun sinks into the cradle of the horizon—inevitably, unerringly, without fear.

His lips were warm and surprisingly soft, achingly gentle. And if there was hesitation, it went the way of regret. There was room for neither—not in the moment, not in her heart.

Loneliness. It was as much a part of him as it was a part of her. If she'd suspected before, she felt it now. Tasted the depth of it as his mouth moved over hers like a lost memory, bittersweet and beckoning. And all she could think, all she could feel was how completely his lost soul matched her own.

This was honesty. This was need. And as he lifted her, shifted her onto his lap, pressed her hip against the hard ridge of his erection so she could feel what she did to him, she'd accepted it was what she'd wanted all along. She understood he wasn't alone, at least not in his need.

She cupped her palm to the dark stubble of his jaw, felt the give of muscle and bone as he deepened the kiss, wrapped her closer until the ache low in her belly matched the ache in her heart.

She shifted to give him better access as his hand swept up her rib cage to cup and caress her breast. Oh, it felt so right as she arched into him, felt the tension in his big body draw bowstring tight, until she realized it wasn't passion, but pain causing the catch in his breath.

She lifted her head and recognized the lines etched around his closed eyes for what they were.

She slid quickly off his lap. "Your ankle?"

He gritted his teeth. Nodded once.

She dragged the hair away from her face, pressed her palms to her heated cheeks then rose. Without a word, she helped him lie back again, lifted his leg until his ankle was propped back up on the pillows.

"I'll get more ice," she said and hurried to the kitchen.

She quickly refilled the plastic storage bag then rewrapped it in a dry towel. Then she stopped, braced her hands on the kitchen counter and breathed deep.

When she was under control again, she returned to

the living room and repacked his ankle. "I'll get you some more aspirin."

He caught her wrist when she turned to go. "Susannah."

She met his eyes, shook her head. "Don't say it. I already know. I just keep making stupid mistakes, don't I?"

But it hadn't felt like a mistake, she told herself as she changed the sheets on her bed then climbed the stairs to make up one of the beds for herself.

It hadn't felt like a mistake at all.

Eleven

Kissing her had been a mistake. Trav hadn't changed his mind since last night when he'd had a temporary lapse of sanity. Something else hadn't changed. The ever-ready state of his body this morning. Like the famous battery bunny, his erection just kept goin' and goin' and goin'. It would have been funny, if it hadn't been so disgusting.

The bed smelled of her. Everything smelled of her. With his arms crossed behind his head, he lay in her bed and looked around the room. The daylight revealed what the night hadn't. It was more a girl's room than a woman's, but then, she'd been a girl when she'd left.

She was a woman now.

And he ached for her. For more of her mouth. For more of her breast nestled in his hand. He'd wanted to taste her there. He'd wanted to taste every part of her.

He'd heard her moving around upstairs earlier, heard her footfalls descend the steps and knew it wouldn't be long before he'd have to face her again. He shouldn't be here, but for her sake it was best that he was. With the electricity and the phones out he didn't want to leave her alone. Not that he could have made it to his truck anyway.

Not that he could have gotten any farther than the

gorge if he had. He'd watched the bridge float away in his rearview mirror right after he'd crossed it yesterday.

Hell, he couldn't even call anyone to check on his place. His cell phone had evidently fallen out of his pocket when he'd gone down. It was out there somewhere in the mud and the muck. Probably washed into the next county with the bridge.

He turned his head toward the window, listened to the dying remnants of the storm. The rain had dwindled to a soft, steady stream. It streaked down the windows like slow melting wax. The wind had died down as well; the light and sound show appeared to be over.

He jerked his head around at the sound of a soft rap on the door.

"I'm awake," he said and dragged the sheet up to midchest.

"Hi." She peeked her head into the room, carrying a pair of crutches. "I found these in the attic." She walked hesitantly into the room, then leaned them against the bedside table. "I got to thinking about the time Dad broke his ankle, and knowing him, I figured he'd squirreled these crutches away somewhere. Sure enough, they were in the attic. They're probably too short for you, but I can help you adjust them."

"I can get it. Thanks," he added belatedly when her cheerful expression fell.

"How are you feeling?"

"Fine."

"Yeah, and I'll buy that if you shell out for some oceanfront property south of the house. No, really," she said, a small smile tilting one corner of her mouth. "It looks like a lake out there."

"Lot of rain," was all he said. "I hope Sis found some shelter."

"Oh, I should have told you last night. She wandered up to the barn before it started in earnest so I stalled her and the filly. They're doing fine. I checked on them this morning."

"Good." He looked away from her because it was too easy to look *at* her. At the softness surrounding her eyes, at that glossy fall of hair he itched to wrap around his fingers. "That's good."

"Well, um, I hope you can do with a minimum of water. I filled as many pans as I could from what was in the pressure tank, but until the electricity comes back on, there's no way to pump it from the well.

"In the meantime, I've got bacon frying. And eggs. Lots of both. The fridge is still marginally cool inside, but I figure we could be without electricity for a few days and things will start to spoil soon. So I hope you're hungry."

"I could eat," he said. "And after that I'll see if I can get the emergency generator started."

"There's an emergency generator?"

"Vi bought it a couple of years ago for just this kind of thing. It's in the pump house."

"Well, if Vi could start it, I should be able to. You've got no business slipping and sliding out there in that mud. After breakfast, you can tell me what I need to do to get it going."

And with that, she left the bedroom.

She was right about one thing. He had no business slipping and sliding around anywhere near her. The problem was, he couldn't count on his usual tactics to save him. He couldn't ride away on his horse, or pile into his truck and haul ass in the other direction.

Considering the duck-and-run approach had been his best defense to date, it left a helluva hole in his battle plan.

He was swearing through clenched teeth when he hobbled into the kitchen several minutes later, and mumbling under his breath about clumsy, helpless fools.

Clumsy, maybe, Susannah thought, as she glanced over her shoulder to see him standing in the doorway like a big wounded grizzly. But helpless? Never. His pride was working on him, though, so she turned back to the stove rather than subject him to an audience as he clunked his way to the kitchen table.

Possibly the memory of the kiss they shared last night was also giving him a little trouble. She knew it was working on her. She'd turned it over and over in her mind all night, was still having problems with it this morning.

She'd dug up an oversized black T-shirt for him to throw on over the sweats and tossed it on the bed when she'd left him the crutches. As he stood there, barefoot, his bed-mussed hair and his strong cheeks darkened with a heavy morning stubble, he should have looked like a thug, not a man who made her pulse skitter and her face flood with sexual heat. The lingering pain etching white lines around his mouth should have made him look dangerous.

Quite probably, he was—at least for her equilibrium. When she turned to set a plate of bacon on the table and saw the expression in the blue eyes that watched her, the threat to her peace of mind, for sure, was definitely there.

She'd caught him off guard before he'd been able

to hide the hunger in his eyes. And again the thought beckoned. What would it be like to be loved by a man of such powerful emotions? What would it take to make a man like him trust again? And trust, she'd decided in the middle of the night as she'd lain in the upstairs bedroom and listened to the rain on the roof, was definitely an issue in his life. That made it an issue between them.

They ate their breakfast in silence. Afterward, Trav concentrated on giving her concise instructions for starting the generator. He was balanced on the crutches and waiting for her by the kitchen door when the lights came on.

He watched from the doorway as she sloughed across the muddy driveway covered from the top of her head to mid-calf in a drab gray poncho. The rubber boots she wore must have weighed ten pounds each. When she hit the porch steps and shoved the hood off her head, she was beaming in triumph.

"Just call me Ace." She toed off the boots by the back door and slipped out of the poncho. "As in mechanic," she added with a grin, shaking her hair free from the knot she'd bunched it in at her nape to keep it dry.

And as he watched the mahogany silk slide across her shoulders, the throbbing in his ankle paled compared to the attention another part of his anatomy demanded.

He wanted her, was drawn to her in ways he didn't understand. Whether it was a result of too many years of denying his needs, too many lonely nights or their forced proximity, he didn't know. No longer cared. It simply was.

He gave up the fight then. Right, wrong. The lines blurred, then disappeared altogether in the utter urgency of his need. He snagged her wrist when she walked by him.

She stopped, swallowed. Didn't say a word. The pulse beneath his fingers fluttered wildly.

He whispered her name. After a long moment, she lifted her head and looked at him. In her eyes, he saw the same fierce longing that burned inside him. In her eyes, he saw surrender.

Without a word, she led him to her bedroom. Morning light spilled into the room through a veil of misty rain as she reached for his crutches then set them aside. He eased onto the bed and sat, eyes locked on her face as she moved between his spread thighs, grasped the hem of the T-shirt and lifted it over his head.

Time, like thought, yielded to this one moment as with no sound, but the slip and glide of soft cotton over softer flesh, she eased her own T-shirt over her head.

He swallowed hard, lost in the sight of her. Soft. Fragrant. Woman. He had to touch her, found his fingers unsteady as he brushed them over the fragile framework of her ribs then reached behind her to undo the clasp of her bra.

The sensations that gripped him were thick in his chest, primal in demand. This was woman in the most elemental sense of the word. Her breasts were heavy, ripe, the pale flesh lightly traced with faint, blue veins just beneath her skin. Her areolas were dusky brown at the center, fanning outward to a delicate coral pink. He reveled in the utter femaleness of her, the incredible textures. He pressed his face between her breasts,

rubbed his cheek against her giving heat, and the unbelievable tension inside him uncoiled in a slow, healing sigh.

She touched her hand to his hair, asked with the
slightest arch of her back for his mouth, for his lips,
for his tongue. He bussed his nose around the velvet
tip of her nipple, caressed her with his breath until
she shivered, then found her with his mouth and
gently suckled.

It was more than sexual, the need that simmered
and burned low in his gut. It was more basic than
lust, more elemental. The heaviness of her breast, the
resilient heat of her skin filling his mouth, filling his
senses, represented the softness he'd been missing in
his life. The subtle sounds she made as she cradled
his head in her hands told him she needed this, too.
This give and take, this tactile reminder that all souls,
especially lost souls, could find sweet healing in each
other.

"No apologies," she whispered, moving with him
as he shifted and reclined on his back in the center
of the bed. "No regrets. It's the only promise I need
from you."

"No apologies," he echoed in a harsh whisper as
he watched her slip out of her shorts and panties. "No
regrets."

He lifted his hips to help her slide the sweats down
his legs and toss them, forgotten, on the floor. She
moved over him then, all silken skin, swaying breasts,
pliant heat.

"Promise me," she insisted in a husky whisper as
she straddled him then hovered on her hands and
knees above him.

He promised. He'd promise anything as he lifted

his head, caught the tip of her breast hungrily in his mouth, then let go on a groan as she stood back on her knees, took him in her hands and guided him to the pulsing center of her.

There was nothing but sensation then. Satin-slick. Enveloping wetness. He could die right now. Right in this moment, he could die with no regrets. She was so tight as she took him deep, her hips pliant where his fingers clutched and encouraged, lifted and settled.

She was the fulfillment of a hundred empty promises. He lost himself in her, as she lost herself in him. Her hair brushed against his chest, feathered across his mouth as she moved above him. He felt cocooned in a perfect web of seduction, as sensation built and pleasure spiked and the only name he could give the feeling was hers.

Too soon, he felt her body quicken, heard her gasping sob of pleasure as she peaked, convulsed then poured her release around him like molten gold.

In this one suspended moment, she was the difference he'd needed in his life and he was the difference in hers. And as he rose to his own peak, where all was lost and all was found, making a difference was the only thing that mattered. Making a difference to someone. Feeling something other than emptiness with someone. Mattering to someone.

It had been so long, he thought as he went the same way she had. So long. If it had ever been like this at all.

The sweet press of her breasts against his chest. The tangle of hair draped across his throat. The gentle silk of her thighs bracketing his hips.

Trav was aware of it all on a peripheral level as he

drifted in a haze of oblivion that felt like the aftermath of so much more than sex. The part of his brain that still shied from such notions warned him away from believing it now.

He opened his eyes, touched a hand to her hair and felt her stir lazily. A soft sigh whispered across his shoulder and he wondered if she was as comfortable as he felt with her warmth pouring over him. With him still buried inside her.

And then reality set in. He'd known it would. He'd known life would intrude and force him to own up to what he'd just let happen. He'd used her.

The regrets, the second thoughts were with him now. In spades. Even though he'd promised her.

He covered his eyes with his arm. What had he done? To himself? To her? And then he felt it. A little ripple of movement against his stomach where her abdomen pressed against him.

The baby.

A maelstrom of emotions roiled through him. Another life, another heartbeat filled the bedroom, filled her body.

A baby.

He'd wanted that once. Children. He'd wanted it all, including the happily ever after. For the past three years, though, all he'd wanted was to survive. And now he'd just made love to a woman who'd bear another man's child.

What did that make him? What did that make her?

The same person she'd been before he'd taken her. Young, stubborn, naive.

Strong.

Of all the labels he wanted to pin on her, that was

the one that stuck. She was strong and so much more than he'd given her credit for being.

She stirred, sighed, lifted her head.

"No guilt," she whispered softly, her blue eyes slumberous and satisfied and intense on his as if reading his mind. "You didn't use me any more than I used you. Besides," she murmured on a yawn so sleepy he wondered if she was aware she'd spoken aloud, "getting used by men is what I do best."

It made him angry suddenly that she so easily let herself fall into that trap. That she sold herself short and in the process made him feel small.

He needed to leave. Now.

But then she touched him, all soft, sleek hands and warm, giving body.

And he submitted again. Surrendered again. And for another suspended moment in time, he was perfectly content to let her use him up.

Susannah left him sleeping. She cleaned up the kitchen, slogged out to the barn to do the chores, then took a shower. She was fussing over Boomer and Sooner, who both looked like they felt neglected, when she heard the clunk of his crutches as he headed down the hall for the bathroom.

His clothes were in the washer with hers when he thumped out to the sofa, smelling like her soap and shampoo and dressed again in his borrowed T-shirt and sweats.

She looked up from the chair as he set the crutches aside. Smiling carefully, she nodded toward the glass of tea she'd set within his reach. "It's not ice cold, but it's wet."

He nodded. "Thanks."

He'd removed the gauze wrap from his head when he'd showered and looked marginally less like a Civil War soldier limping home from battle.

"How's the head?"

"Not bad. Swelling's down. Stopped bleeding."

"Want some help with that?" she asked with a nod toward the compression wrap he brought with him and hung over his shoulder.

"That'd be good. Yeah. It seems to help."

"So would some ice. We should have some soon."

"And then we'd better shut off the generator until it gets dark, conserve the gas in case the power's off for a while yet."

She wondered how he felt about the possibility of being stranded here with her for another day or two. She wondered how she felt about it, then decided it was best not to explore it too deeply. Some things, she'd learned, were best dealt with in the moment. This was one of those things.

They settled in then, him lying down with his foot up, her thumbing through a magazine. It was months old, but gave her something to do with her hands. Sitting here together might have felt comfortable, restful even, if not for what lay unspoken between them.

Still, she didn't want to talk about what they'd shared in her bed. It was too special, too important to her to ruin with words. Or with regrets and she suspected he had them.

"Are you, um, okay?" he asked into her thoughtful silence.

For some reason his question made her smile—and feel like teasing. Physically, she felt loose and lush and sort of tingling with an inner glow. "Never better. And you?"

His gaze slid to hers. When he saw her grin and the little flicker of lingering sexual heat, he shook his head. Then he smiled. "Relaxed," he said, then smiled again. "I'm feeling very, *very* relaxed," he added and all she could do was stare.

The transformation his smile made was stunning. Stone-faced and somber, he was dramatically attractive. Sloe-eyed and smiling, he was devastating.

"What?" he asked, his quick scowl returning.

She shook her head. "Sorry. I didn't mean to stare. But do you realize that's the first time I've ever seen you smile?"

In answer, he grunted.

"You ought to do it more often."

He grunted again and this time she laughed. "It's hard for you to let down your guard, isn't it?"

"Yeah, well, I'm a slow learner, but I learn my lessons well."

"And you've learned you need to keep your guard up around me?"

"Not you," he said and she could see in his eyes the surprise when he realized he meant it. But he didn't elaborate.

She decided she would. "There are a lot of lessons to learn in this old world."

"Spoken like an ancient sage."

She met his hard stare without blinking. "Age is relative. Experience is what counts." She looked at him reclining there, staring not at her now, but at his hands. "Something tells me we've both had our fair share of bad ones."

He did look at her then. At her face, then lower, to

her abdomen. "Was the guy who did that one of them?"

She smiled tightly. "He was a boy. I'd wanted him to be a man. I'd wanted to matter. Rodeo mattered more. End of story."

A long silence passed. "Did you love him?"

It stunned her that he'd asked the question. Not because she didn't know how to answer, but because he was interested enough to ask.

"I wanted to." She shook her head. "But then, I wanted to love every one of those wild boys who convinced me I mattered. That's where it always got sticky. Turns out I only mattered for the short go." She shrugged, accepting. "I guess that's what happens when you're—how does the song go?—looking for love in all the wrong places?"

His jaw clenched. And then her heart stuttered and she knew she was going to stick her neck out and ask. "What about you? Did you love her?"

His head whipped around, his eyes cutting into hers. He opened his mouth then shut it, working his jaw. "Yeah," he said after the moment it took for him to decide to level with her, to admit there had been a woman in his life.

"What happened?" She held her breath, waited, wondered if she'd gone too far.

"She got pregnant."

Confusion pinched her brows while a sharp spear of pain lanced through her. "And you didn't want the baby?"

He let his head fall back on the pillow she'd propped behind his shoulders and covered his eyes with his forearm. "I wanted *our* baby. And that was the problem. It wasn't mine."

"Travis." His name whispered out on a sigh filled with compassion.

He lifted his arm, stretched it toward the ceiling, watched his fingers as he flexed them. "You marry a woman, love her, make plans. You build a practice with your best friend. Love him like a brother. Make more plans. What you don't plan on is finding them in bed together. What you don't plan on is a rage so strong, so consuming that it overrules everything you abhor."

She swallowed, felt the tears well then trickle down her cheeks.

"I beat the hell out of him. Almost killed him." He lowered his hand. Stared into space and repeated on a guilt-ridden breath, "Almost killed him."

Betrayal. Shame. Horror over what he'd done, this man who showed such gentleness and compassion with animals. What his actions cost him in terms of his sense of self must be immeasurable. She felt the pain of it pour out of him and went to him, knelt beside him on the floor, laid her head on his chest. Just to touch him. Just to let him know she was there.

His arm hovered above her shoulders and finally settled. As he ran his hand in a slow caress over her hair, she felt the need in him.

"I'm so sorry."

His hand stopped.

She lifted her head, rose to her knees and kissed him. "So, so sorry."

She couldn't bear the way his face had closed up. Couldn't bear to know he was closing up inside again, as well. Sure, she knew what they were to each other—two lonely people finding solace in the rain. But in this moment she didn't care that there wasn't more, would probably never be more. She just wanted to make his hurt go away.

She kissed him again, lingering over his mouth, then kissed a slow path across his jaw, licked her way down his throat. Her fingers found the drawstring on the waistband of his sweats and tugged it free.

"Susannah." His throat convulsed as she pressed a kiss there then moved lower to swirl her tongue around the indentation of his navel. His muscles constricted; he fisted a hand in her hair. "Susannah."

"Shush," she murmured, working the loose cotton down his hips, taking him in her hand, touching him with her tongue. "Let me."

Trav breathed deep, shifted, trying not to wake her. She was sleeping now. On top of him. On the sofa where moments before she'd given him the most intimate, most generous gift.

Elena, in the fifteen years they'd been together, had never, ever given him anything that even remotely compared. What Susannah had done to him went far beyond sex. It was the selflessness of the act. It was the tears trailing down her cheeks when she took him in her mouth. The look in her eyes after he'd come. Her refusal to let him pleasure her in return. She'd humbled him.

He pressed a kiss to the top of her head, trailed the silk of her hair through her fingers.

"Hmm. That feels good." She stretched like a contented cat.

"I could make you feel better."

Her smile stirred the fine hair on his chest near his collarbone. "I couldn't possibly feel any better."

She was quiet for a time, then the fingers she'd

been drifting over his ribs stilled. "Talk to me. Tell me something about Vi. Tell me how you got to know her."

He didn't know how much time passed then as they lay on the sofa and he talked. About Vi. About how, despite their age difference, they somehow managed to connect.

"We were both loners, yet we found some common ground as we worked side by side on the range." He thought back to their endless discussions on market trends, grazing management, breeding.

"We pulled calves together and on one unplanned, but momentous occasion, we killed a fifth of Jack Daniels together."

"You liked each other," she concluded.

"Yeah. And we respected each other, knew when to back off, when not to pry."

"Am I prying now?" she asked quietly.

He covered her hand and squeezed. "No. You're not prying. But you need to know something. I'm surprised you haven't already heard it. I did some time over...well, I told you. I really did nearly kill him."

She didn't say anything, but the silence wasn't judgmental.

"I would have had a stiffer sentence, but he wouldn't testify against me. Guess he felt he owed me that."

"And maybe he was basically a good man who knew he'd made a really bad mistake."

"Yeah," he said and knew it was true. He still didn't know what had happened with his marriage, figured he never would.

She lifted her head. Smiled. "Well, we really aren't

so different, you and I, are we? We've both got poor judgment and bad luck when it comes to the opposite sex.''

He grimaced on a caught breath.

''What the matter? Am I getting too heavy for you?'' she asked in alarm when he shifted his hips.

She wasn't too heavy. But she'd gotten so damn close to what he was about. Who he was. Closer than he'd let anyone get to him in a very long time.

He felt a small flicker of panic, decided it was time to back away. ''Let's go back in the bedroom. There's something I want to show you.''

Because she smiled when he said it, he laughed. When they finally made it to the bedroom he did show her something. He showed her how gorgeous her legs looked draped over his shoulders; he showed her a little bit of the heaven she'd shown him.

''Guess we're reconnected to civilization,'' Susannah said when the phone rang about four-thirty that afternoon.

It was Clarence, and he was worried about her.

''Sounds like the county road crew has managed to jury-rig a passable, but temporary bridge over the washout.''

She'd already figured as much. She'd heard the distant grumble of diesel engines a couple of hours ago. And she'd known her time with Travis was close to an end.

His long silence and somber eyes told her she was right. When he finally spoke, she was prepared for what happened next.

''I need to get back. Check on things.''

She nodded. ''I know.''

A little while later he was gone. No long goodbyes. No "I'll be back tonight." No "Well, what happens now?"

Susannah knew what happened now. Nothing. She knew the drill. Unlike the others, Travis Dean was not a love-'em-and-leave-'em kind of guy. But he was leaving anyway, and she understood why.

Whether he was still mired in his anger over his wife's betrayal, or had simply decided it wasn't worth the effort, he wasn't ready to open himself up to love a woman again. Every woman who crossed his path was going to pay for his wife's sins. It didn't matter that what they'd shared was special. It was a moment in time and she was pragmatic enough to realize the moment was over.

She stood at the window watching his truck pull out of the lane. She'd fallen in lust with a string of cowboys, fallen in hope that one of them would love her. But she'd never fallen in love. Not until now.

She suspected it had happened the very first day she'd seen him, scowling and sincere in his grief over Vi's death, grim and growling over her determination to stay. Compassionate and patient with Sooner.

She loved him—and he didn't want her any more than the others had.

"Can't say your luck isn't holding," she said to herself as she wandered back into the den. "Too bad most of it is bad."

Needing to take her mind off what wasn't going to happen between them, she dug the diaries out from under the attic step and resumed her work decoding them.

Twelve

The children were impossible not to love and while I understood the necessity of Mr. Croft from Medusa arriving within days of their birth to check out the progress of the experiment, I didn't like the hungry way he eyed my babies. To him, they were scientific research, nothing more. With each day it became more apparent that Agnes and Oliver regarded them in the same way.

As the months passed, it became increasingly harder for me to turn them over to the cold, clinical scientists who only handled them in the interest of running their tests. It wasn't that they were cruel. They had too much time invested to treat my babies with anything other than the utmost care. Still, I felt a cold chill when they remarked on how anxious they were to see if the children would rise to their full potential. Jake had been engineered to possess extraordinary mathematical and pecuniary skills, and Grace was given amazing powers to process signs and symbols, enabling her to break any code or solve any puzzle, in addition to making her an exceptional linguist.

Only Henry seemed to regard the children as I did. Lovingly, adoringly. And it was during this time I began to sense Henry watching me through different eyes, as well. His heart had softened, opened, and I secretly reveled in the small attentions he began to show me. I didn't let him know I'd noticed, of course. He would have withdrawn immediately and I couldn't take a chance he'd break the bond he'd forged with our children. They needed him. Even then something inside me feared for their safety.

Time went by so quickly. Suddenly, they were two years old and both Jake and Grace spoke clearly in full sentences and polysyllabic words. Grace spoke several languages and put together thousand-piece puzzles. It was a continuous challenge to keep her active and vital mind occupied. At twenty-four months Jake could add, subtract, multiply and divide large sums in his head. Every day when we spent time in the playroom, he'd build amazingly complex structures with his Lego. About the only true challenge for either of them was when they faced off with each other for a game of chess. Talk about competitive spirits!

Aside from their enhanced skills, however, they were still toddlers in every other sense of the word. They loved hugs and kisses; they cried when they were angry, laughed when something tickled them. We adored them, Henry and I. I adore them still and I pray they are whole and happy even as the world assumes them dead...as they have been dead to me for all these years....

Enthralled, Susannah glanced at the clock, shook her head at the late hour and kept working. She scanned several pages then skipped ahead when she realized Vi was about to give birth to yet three more children less than three years after Jake and Grace were born.

When Jake and Grace were little more than two

years old, I was impregnated with eggs fertilized in-vitro with Henry's genetically enhanced sperm. Again, only three of the five eggs developed into embryos, but we were very excited and encouraged by the extent of the success.

The pregnancy was unremarkable until my seventh month when something happened that was to forever change things between Henry and me. I stumbled on the stairs and took a horrible fall. Even as Henry rushed me to the hospital, my concern was for the babies. Henry's concern was for me. It was his tender care that pulled me through. He nursed me through a broken ankle, two broken ribs and an extensive cut on my forehead. The pain was incredible, the scar on my face nasty. I was restricted to bed for the rest of the pregnancy. My poor children didn't understand what had happened to Mommy and asked a million questions.

Despite the fall, my babies, thank God, were fine. And Henry— I don't even know how to relate the change that came over him. Only later did he confess that it was when I lay near death that he realized he truly loved me and would do anything for me.

I delivered with no difficulty two months later and, oh, what miracles these children were. Mark was physically gifted with superhuman strength. Faith was engineered to be a physician and diagnostician, and Gideon was programmed for technological comprehension. My love for them was unconditional.

The other miracle was that Henry had come to love not only the babies, but me, as well. I had suspected, but had never dreamed that shortly after the birth, he would surprise me with a gold-and-ruby ring. The day he placed it on my finger and asked me to place an identical ring on his was the day I considered us married. Traditional? No. Not even consummated. But it was enough for me. I'd loved him for so long. Even though he couldn't verbalize his feelings for me, it was enough, until finally one night he came to my bed.

My experiences in foster homes and one very unfortunate incident in college had made me wary of physical intimacies between a man and a woman. But Henry was so patient, so loving and tender, I knew without a doubt he had truly come to love me in every sense of the word.

Years then passed so quickly as we became a family. Life seemed almost idyllic, but it was only an illusion. Henry shared his deepest fears with me. He believed what I had suspected for several years...and it was then I understood I'd been deluding myself into believing we could ever be safe....

Susannah was aware that she was almost through the diaries now. She knew the last pages would finally reveal the details leading to Vi's death. More than curiosity made her continue. She owed it to Vi to finish this. With the rings clutched in her hand, she went back to work.

For some time I had suspected Agnes and Oliver had been in collusion with Willard Croft over the future of my children. For some time I'd feared Henry's life may be in danger. Everything Henry confided to me confirmed I had reason to be afraid.

He told me that when I'd fallen they had been willing—even eager—to let me bleed to death then and there. They'd encouraged Henry to simply help them deliver the babies and refuse medical attention for me. I was no longer necessary, it seemed. It was then that Henry began to fear for all of our lives.

Nearly ten uneasy years passed as Henry played a cat-and-mouse game with his research, hiding his notes, correctly surmising that as long as Croft and Agnes and Oliver didn't have the necessary scientific notes and details, he was indispensable. My situation was a little more precarious and we constantly covered each other's backs to avoid the worst. Oliver and Agnes had had enough of Henry's secrecy, however. They became impatient, no longer content to work in his shadow or wait to discover his notes.

I cannot easily relate what happened next. I cannot bear to think past the cold, blunt facts and must relate them the same way or I will not be able to get through this.

I suspected then and became sure later. They killed him. In cold blood. Without remorse. They laid in wait for him when he jogged as he always jogged along the surf every morning. He was in his forties, robust and healthy, when they bludgeoned the husband of my heart to death. They tossed him into the tide and allowed the police to assume he'd drowned after being caught and pulled into the rocks by an undertow.

As devastated as I was, I saw through their lies. They knew I would go to the police, so they overpowered me, drugged me. Worse, they took my children from me to the house nearby where Oliver and Agnes had moved along with a man named Victor Prego, the tutor Medusa had hired for the children.

Victor stayed with me at Belle Terre and from what I gather, kept me drugged for several days so Oliver and Agnes could hypnotize my children and erase their memories of both Henry and me. Jake and Grace, Mark, Faith and Gideon were under the control of monsters!

Only one thing kept them from killing me, too. They hadn't been able to find Henry's notes on Code Proteus. Without the notes, they were nothing and could not proceed with whatever diabolical schemes they had in the works. They assumed correctly that I had access to the priceless research. They also assumed they would eventually drag the information out of me. They had my children, after all. They knew I would have done anything to save them—even betray Henry's secret research and knowingly let it fall into these fiends' hands.

But I fought them. I don't know how I did it. One night as Victor slept, I dragged myself out of my drugged stupor. I did it for Henry, who was gone. I did it for my children, whom I could not allow to be used like lab rats. I crawled from the bed, found the drugs Victor had used on me and injected him. I may have killed him. I don't know. To this day, I don't care. I only cared about getting my children away from these people.

Henry and I had prepared for such an emergency, assuming something horrible was in the offing. We'd hidden an emergency pack with money and passports, false IDs and birth certificates for all of us. Also in the pack were the secret tapes containing all of Henry's notes on his genetic research.

As part of our escape plan, we'd hidden a van in a garage a mile away from Belle Terre. I found my way to it that night then went to rescue my children.

It was horrible. I'd never felt such fear as I sneaked into Oliver and Agnes's bedroom and injected them with the same drug I'd used on Victor. And then I searched.

I found Jake first. He was sleeping like an angel when I woke him and frightened him half to death. He didn't know me. He'd been hypnotized and brainwashed to the point where he—my own child—didn't know me. No matter how I pleaded and tried to explain, he would not come with me willingly. I had no choice. God forgive me, I had no choice.

I wrestled him to his bed, muffled his small cries and injected him, praying I did not overdose him. Then I repeated the process with the other four, crying as I did it, dragging them one by one out to the van, fearful of Agnes and Oliver waking and catching me before I got them safely away.

I almost made it. I almost got them all out of that horrible place. But when I went back for Gideon, Agnes had fought off the effects of the drug. She was weaving on her feet and barely conscious as she fired a gun. I heard a scream. I will always hear that scream. It was Gideon. My child. She'd aimed for me and shot my child, and I knew in that moment he was lost to me forever. Yet I tried. I made one last desperate lunge for Gideon as he fell. And lay there. Still as stone, his blood seeping along with his life onto the floor.

I couldn't save him. I couldn't help him then. He was gone. So I ran to save the others, sobbing, fighting hysteria and fate as Agnes's gun evidently jammed when she stumbled across the room after me. All I could do was run to save the rest of my children before she shot me, too, and all would be lost.

The night is still a blur in my mind. I remember shadows and headlights and rain and tears clouding my vision as I raced through the night to seek shelter with Leo Doppler, Henry's old friend. Leo's cottage was on a remote island in the ocean off Georgia. Henry had confided to Leo that we may need his help one day. Little did we know it would be under such dire circumstances.

God bless Leo. He used his psychology training to hypnotize the children again to make them trust me as well as instill the importance of never, ever contacting Agnes and Oliver in the future. Everything happened very fast then. We arranged for the children to be adopted, as we knew they would never be safe with me. Jake would go to a family in Dallas, Grace to San Francisco. Faith's new home would be Minneapolis while Mark would go to Baltimore.

I cannot express the pain. I knew I would never see them again, but I'd saved them—at least I'd saved four of them—and that was all that mattered. It had to matter. I would kill them and myself before I would willingly surrender them to Medusa and Croft and Agnes and Oliver.

But my work was not yet finished. Medusa had to believe we were dead, so Leo and I staged a boat accident and made sure there were witnesses. With the children on board, I piloted a small craft out into the bay, then stopped as if we were having engine trouble. One by one I had the children slip over the side and swim to Leo's boat, which was hidden from view of the shoreline. Grace and I were the last to leave before I hit the explosive device Leo had rigged. We clung to each other as the boat blew up in a ball of flames and flying debris.

Two days later, my babies were gone—once again hypnotized by Leo and dispatched to their adoptive homes with no memories of their life or their ordeal. It was the only way to ensure their safety.

And I was alone again.

My children were safe. At least four of my children were safe. I prayed Gideon was alive, but in my heart I knew he was gone. I had to look past my failings and focus on the importance of convincing Medusa they were all dead. I had no doubt they had found the computer tapes I'd planted in the van. They were dummy tapes, of course, designed to make them think they were Henry's notes when in fact the tapes were filled with false equations and written in such a complicated computer code it would take them months, possibly years to break it before they realized they'd been duped. Since I had also wiped the computers clean at Belle Terre before I left, Henry's notes were safe with me. And I vowed with my life that no one would get them unless I decided to make them available.

I find I must stop for a while. The memories are more painful than I can endure....

Susannah sat for a long time reading and rereading every detail. Vi's story had pulled her back in time into a past of passion and pain, unspeakable sins and incredible truths. How brave she'd been. How much she'd suffered. Susannah had wondered about the scar on Vi's forehead, but she'd never asked, sensing Vi's sensitivity even as an eleven-year-old child still mourning the loss of her mother.

Like Vi, she'd reached the level of her endurance. She couldn't read anymore. She went to bed. Thinking about Vi. Thinking about Travis. They'd both endured so much.

Susannah still felt emotionally spent the next morning when she got up. For the baby's sake, she made

herself stay away from the diaries all day. She did
chores, she did laundry, baked a cake. Anything to
keep her mind occupied. If she let it drift, her
thoughts scattered too far, too wide. She thought too
much. About Vi. About Travis. It always came back
to Travis.

She knew better than to watch for him, and yet, her
gaze kept straying toward the driveway, where it
would pause on the fallen cottonwood. And she
would picture him then, his head bleeding, his ankle
swollen and discolored. And she would wonder how
he was.

He'd be fine. He would heal. He was strong.

She only hoped she was as strong as she needed to
be to work with him and accept whatever he decided
was going to be between them. He cared about her.
But he didn't love her. Nor did she expect him to.

Could she be content with that? Could she be content being his partner and his sometime lover and
know he could never offer her more than that?

She didn't know. She just didn't know.

It was almost sunset when his pickup pulled into
her drive. She watched him through the kitchen window, her heart in her throat, and willed herself to
settle down. To stop the second guesses before they
started. Of course he'd come back. The Rocking H
was partly his now. He'd need to check on things.
He'd need to see her, she dared to hope as he swung
out of the truck and hobbled on his crutches toward
the house.

"Hi," she said, opening the door, working for a
casual smile and hoping her heart didn't show through
her eyes.

"Yeah. Hi."

"How...how are you doing?"

He shrugged. "Fine. Was on my ankle a little too much today so I'm back to using these."

"Were things okay at home?"

He nodded. "We got by without too much damage."

She nodded, then felt the hot burn of tears in her eyes. They came out of nowhere. She couldn't stop them or the sobs that suddenly racked her body.

The next thing she knew, she was wrapped in his arms. Warm and protected. Steadied and cared for.

And nothing mattered, but the moment and the fact that he held her.

Travis wasn't sure what he'd seen in her eyes before she'd crumbled. Welcome. Tension. Uncertainty. He'd gone to her automatically, every protective gene in his body springing to red alert.

And then it hit him.

"The baby?" He was astounded at how panicked he felt. "Has something happened to the baby?"

"No. No," she managed between tears. "The baby's fine. I'm fine. I don't know what's wrong with me. Hormones, maybe?" she suggested on a shaky laugh. "Or the storm. I realize how much worse it could have been."

"It's all right. You're all right," he assured her, running his hands up and down her back.

Against him, he felt her gather herself, try to pull it together, then give up the fight. "I'm sorry. I told myself I wouldn't ask."

"Ask," he said simply.

"Stay." She lifted her head, met his eyes. "Just tonight. Stay and hold me. I need someone to hold me tonight."

He hadn't come here to crawl back in her bed. At least he told himself he was above that. And he wasn't relieved when she'd made it easy for him to do just that.

But later, in the dark, in her arms, he knew he lied. He needed her—more, maybe, than she seemed to need him. He needed to be over her, under her; he needed to be inside her.

Yet like his own desperation, he recognized hers. It was there in her eyes, in her lovemaking. Because she wanted more from him than he was prepared to give? Because she knew, in her heart, he had nothing but this to give her?

Maybe. Or maybe there was something else. Something she wasn't telling him. Hell, maybe she thought he was the one who was too needy. Maybe she was afraid of pressure from him.

As she slept beside him, the thought of her walking away from him hit him like a gut punch.

He didn't get it. They had no hold on each other. That was the way he wanted it. No commitment, no deeper involvement. Yet he'd be lying if he didn't admit he'd actually found himself looking ahead to the next months, the next year with Susannah. A little dark-haired child always hovered on the fringes of that picture.

He went to sleep seeing it in his mind. He went to sleep with her curled against his side and considered himself lucky. He went to sleep thinking ahead, not back. Maybe it was time to look ahead. Maybe it was time.

Susannah left him sleeping at four in the morning. As deliriously happy as she was that Travis had come to her, as sated as she was from the tender way he'd made love to her, she couldn't get Vi's diaries out of her mind. She'd thought she could wait, thought she could finish them tomorrow, but her sense of urgency had built as the pages yet to be deciphered dwindled.

Turning on a single light in the living room, she sat down with them again. She needed to know how this ended. She needed to know what had happened to Vi.

She'd considered telling Travis about the diaries last night. She wanted to tell him. Yet something held her back. Until she unraveled the entire story, she was afraid to share. She was afraid that when she knew the whole story, the knowledge could possibly place her in danger. If Travis knew, he could possibly be in danger, too.

The next several years are still a blur. I wandered as far away from Georgia as I could get and eventually found myself in the southwestern part of the United States in my effort to disappear. I did not live. I barely existed. I mourned for my children. I mourned for Henry. I agonized over Gideon. I'm not sure why I didn't just end it all. I had nothing; I had no one. Only memories. Only fears.

My body, as much as my mind, finally grew weary of wandering one day and I simply stopped here in Colorado. I worked in town, near the Rocking H for several years. I kept house for people, did odd jobs. I got by. Then one day this sad and lonely man came to me, asked if I'd be willing to keep house for him and care for his eleven-year-old daughter. He broke down and cried as he talked to me.

His wife had died and he was desperate for help with the house, with his daughter. Most of all, though, it was sadly obvious he was desperate for company. I knew his pain. Felt it as keenly as he did. And for that reason, I almost turned him down. Seeing him resurrected so many of my own memories...memories I'd tried desperately to suppress over the years.

I'd been without my Henry and my children for thirteen years. But this man, Dale Hobson, needed me as I had once been needed in my life and in the end I could not say no to him.

It's difficult to say when my compassion for Dale turned to love. It's hard to say when I stopped regarding Susannah as a reminder of the children I'd given up to save and began loving her as my own. The heart is truly the most resilient organ in the human body. And Dale and Susannah helped heal the wounded part of mine. Did I love him as passionately as I loved Henry? No. But I did love him, and Susannah. Oh, how I loved that child.

I miss them. I miss her and only pray she's not lost to me forever as everyone has been lost to me....

Tears streamed down Susannah's cheeks as she thought of Vi's loving attention. There had been good times. When she hadn't been mourning her mother, when she hadn't been acting out her anger, there had been good times.

She had been a child. A child who had stormed out of the house and out of Vi's life when her father died. Four years ago. Four wasted years.

She forced herself to read on. And as she read, she met Travis through Vi's eyes and fell deeper in love.

I received a gift one day. The calves dropped early, too early to avoid one last blast of winter that dropped six inches of snow during the night. I was riding above the frost line, searching a snow-swept slope for babies in trouble, and stumbled over a man.

He was on his knees in the snow. His hands were raw from the cold as they held one of my newborn calves against his body heat and rubbed it down to stimulate circulation.

His name was Travis Dean, and in his eyes I saw a soul as lonely as my own.

Over the next several months, we became friends. We became each other's saviors, yet to this day, we've never asked the other what we'd needed saving from. It wasn't necessary. And that was what made him so special to me....

Susannah decoded several more pages, smiling, sometimes crying at Vi's account of her friendship with Travis. In a way the passages settled her, eased her mind. Vi hadn't been alone. Neither had Travis once they'd found each other. And for the first time she considered there had been a master plan after all. She'd needed time to leave this place and grow. Vi and Travis had needed each other.

And guilt, like grief, lifted a little in the knowledge that fate may have had more of a hand in their lives than any of them could have imagined.

While I always prayed Susannah would return home, life went on. Seasons changed. Memories faded. And then one day, the newspaper tilted the insular world I'd created and set it on its axis....

As she flipped the page she'd just decoded, Susannah realized a newspaper clipping lay between it and the next page of Vi's journal. Her heart stuttered when she read the date. It had been printed less than four months ago. Her fingers were trembling when she set aside her pen and began to scan the article.

Inside sources indicate the World Bank has been the victim of a computer heist in the $350 billion dollar range... It appears to have been a multi-layered and extremely complex plot...ultimately involved a power failure.... The bank's mainframe was corrupted...resulting in the channeling of funds into a series of dummy accounts and phony corporations, the sources of which have not yet been tracked down.... No solid leads on the individual or individuals who perpetrated this crime have been substantiated, but the name Achilles seems to be on the tip of everyone's tongues as speculation runs rampant on how the fallout of this financial crisis will affect worldwide economy.... FBI is among the investigating agencies.... Well-known financial wizard Jake Ingram has also been called in to assist....

Susannah's hand was still shaking as she set the clipping with its photograph of Jake Ingram aside and returned to the journal.

I knew. I knew immediately that Achilles had to be Gideon! Grace and Jake had given him the nickname when he was little, teasing him that his temper would be his Achilles' heel. Gideon was alive. He hadn't died. It had to be him. Only someone who possessed his extraordinary skills could have pulled off a feat of this magnitude.

But why? Why would he have committed such a crime? The answer became suddenly obvious. Croft, Agnes and Oliver had programmed him to do it. They had turned my Gideon into a criminal for their own gain. And now it was Jake, my darling Jake, who would help track him down and bring him to justice. Gideon was his brother and there was no way for him to know.

I have to do something. I must find Jake. Oh, he looks so like his father! I must tell him about Gideon. I must tell him about the other three children before something else horrible happens. If it hasn't happened already. What if they're dead? What if Agnes and Oliver found them?

Suddenly I fear I've been foolish and stupid to have severed my ties with them. Have I been leaving them unprotected and vulnerable, instead of protecting them with my distance? Had Medusa found them? Or, like me, was this the first they've heard of my extraordinary children and are just now coming to the realization they are alive, not dead? There are so many questions. And no true answers. Jake. I must find Jake. My time and theirs, I fear, is running short.

This must be why I've sensed for several months that something—something horrible or wonderful—was about to happen.

My children. My God. I may see my children again....

Susannah stared at the page in her hand. That was it. She'd decoded the last page, and like Vi, she still had a hundred questions. What happened next? Had Vi found Jake? Is that who she'd gone to see when she left on her trips? Was it because of her discoveries she was dead? Could there be any doubt it was Agnes and Oliver or perhaps even Croft or someone else from Medusa who had killed her?

She looked down at the rings hanging from the gold chain, lifted them, turned them over in her palm, searching—in vain, she knew—for some additional clue. Light refracted from the table lamp onto the inside of the rings. She squinted, brought them closer and discovered a scratch on the inside of the larger ring that she now knew was Henry's.

With a little quickening in her heart, she lifted the chain over her neck, studied it in more detail. It wasn't a scratch after all. It was an engraving. She moved quickly through the house to the kitchen, surprised to see the sun rising and spilling warmth into the morning. Absently, she reached in the tool drawer, fished around until she found the magnifying glass. Taking the ring to the light, she held it under the glass.

"BLUEWATER," she whispered aloud. Yes. It definitely, read: BLUEWATER. But there was more. A series of numbers followed the word. More code? She copied them onto paper. Nothing. She couldn't come up with any combination to make it work. If it was code, it wasn't the one Vi had taught her.

She couldn't imagine what the numbers meant. But suddenly she understood. These rings with their engraved letters and numbers, coupled with Vi's diaries, held the key to Vi's death—and quite possibly to the lives of Vi's five children.

It was time, she decided, to do something. It was time to quit denying the truth of Vi's diaries and trust that Vi knew what she was doing if and when she contacted Jake Ingram. She walked back into the living room and reviewed the newspaper article, noticing for the first time what appeared to be a phone number written in pencil on the bottom of the page. Jake's? There was only one way to find out.

Her hand trembled as she punched in the number. She sat in tense silence, clutching the receiver to her ear, listening to it ring, praying she wasn't placing her life or her baby's life in danger.

Thirteen

Travis walked into the kitchen to see Susannah on the phone. Unaware that he was standing behind her, she spoke quietly, casting nervous glances at the clock. It was barely 5:00 a.m.

"Yes, Jake. I'll meet you there. Tomorrow. One o'clock. Yes. I'll see you then."

Jake. She was meeting someone named Jake tomorrow. Something inside him knotted. Something inside him closed off. He shifted his weight and a floorboard creaked. She spun around as if she'd been caught committing a crime.

And that was when he knew. His gaze flicked to her abdomen then back to her face. Jake. So that was the bastard's name.

And she was meeting him tomorrow.

The fact spun around in his mind until he couldn't think straight. He watched her face as she hung up the phone, dropping it like it was a piece of contraband she had no business holding.

She ducked her head, forced a smile. "That...was an old friend. He's...passing through tomorrow and wanted to meet me...in town."

She was lying. He'd heard enough lies from Elena to recognize a whopper. But it wasn't until she looked away from him, unable to meet his eyes, that he headed for the door, damning himself for a fool.

He didn't want to think. He just wanted out of there. "I've got to be going."

And yet he hesitated with his hand on the knob. Waited for more explanation. Waited for nothing. He jerked the door open, then heard her say his name.

"Travis?"

He didn't turn around. He knew if he did she'd read the look on his face for what it was. Desperation. He was desperate for her to give him a reason to stay.

Several seconds passed before he accepted it wasn't going to happen. She didn't know what to say to him, either.

Without another word, he walked out the door.

It was her life, not his. And he'd been worse than a fool when he'd started thinking he might have a place in it.

In Dallas, Texas, Jake Ingram stared at the phone long after the connection with Susannah Hobson was broken.

Dead. Violet was dead.

He closed his eyes. My God. He'd only just met her. She'd given up so much for him and the other four. Now she was dead because of her sacrifice. He dragged his hands through his hair unable to fully assimilate the news as his fiancée, Tara Linden, entered the room.

She stopped, frowned. "You okay?"

"No." He let out a deep breath. "I'm not okay."

Tara watched him expectantly; impatience undercut the compassion in her eyes.

He'd like to tell her the truth—about everything. About his past. About the phone call he'd just received from Violet Vaughn Hobson's stepdaughter.

Yeah. He'd like to tell her, but…it was too much.
Too many unanswered questions. Too much danger.

Violet. His birth mother. Dead. It all seemed surreal, unbelievable.

"Jake?"

He glanced over his shoulder and saw the concern
in Tara's eyes. "I'm sorry. I just got some bad
news."

"Anything I can help with?"

He shook his head. "It's confidential. I really can't
elaborate."

"Can't or won't?"

More than disappointment added an edge to her
biting reply. She was angry.

"Tara, I'm sorry. You're going to have to trust me
on this."

"Lot of that going around these days. Trusting
you."

She turned and walked out of the room. She was
running out of patience with him. He didn't blame
her. He'd been so preoccupied—both with work and
the past that had been unfolding—that he'd been ne-
glecting her. She had a right to feel hurt. But their
problems would have to wait. More lives could be on
the line.

He hesitated, then picked up the phone and dialed.
He had business obligations to tie up today, but he'd
promised Susannah Hobson he'd meet her in Colorado tomorrow. She had information. Information she
didn't feel comfortable sending through the mail. He
needed to get there. He needed anything she had.
Anything that might contain the clues he needed to
unravel this entire mess.

* * *

Susannah clutched her arms around her waist and watched Travis go. She'd wanted to tell him. She'd wanted to tell him the whole convoluted story. But she was afraid. Afraid she might endanger Jake and his brothers and sisters, possibly herself and the baby and even Travis.

He'd been hurt by her silence. The pain had been there, carved on the face she loved, turning it hard again, closing him off.

When this was over, she would tell him. She prayed it would be over soon. For now all she could do was hope for the best.

Her palms were damp as she walked to the den and lifted the chain holding the rings over her head. She placed them carefully in the box with Vi's decoded journals and hid them under the attic step. Then she did everything in her power to keep from crawling out of her skin as she waited for tomorrow to come.

Tomorrow. This would all be over tomorrow. At least she hoped it would be.

She didn't sleep that night. At one the next day she felt the effects. Her fingers were stiff and clammy wrapped around the steering wheel as she waited at the far end of the parking lot at the high school football field where she'd arranged to meet him. She hadn't wanted to meet Jake at the Rocking H. She hadn't wanted him to bring the danger to her home.

When a car pulled up, she knew this was it. The dark haired man behind the wheel looked her way, nodded.

He had Vi's blue eyes.

With a slow breath of relief, she got out of the car, retrieved the box of journals from the trunk and prayed he hadn't been followed.

* * *

Alone in first-class later that day, Jake let his head fall against the headrest as the flight attendant made the announcement to prepare for landing in Dallas. He'd met with Susannah Hobson mere hours ago in Colorado. He'd just read the last of her notes on Violet's diaries. And was stunned.

Violet had intended to tell him all of this when they'd met in D.C., but she'd been afraid, skittish, and before she'd disclosed any information, she'd run. Run to her death.

What Susannah had shared was… Well, it was all too much to absorb. Yet one fact was unalterable. He had to get this information to his sister, Gretchen. He had to show his sister the rings.

He thought back to his conversation with Susannah.

"Do the engravings mean anything to you?" he'd asked.

"Nothing. I was hoping you'd know."

He'd looked at her then. At this strong woman who had stuck her neck out for him, for Violet and her memory.

"She'd intended to tell me where she'd hidden Henry's notes on Code Proteus, but something spooked her and she ran before she could finish."

"She ran home," Susannah had said gravely. "And they followed her."

"They," he'd repeated. "Whoever they are. Croft? Someone else from Medusa? God. Will we ever know?"

"Maybe the engravings will hold the answer."

He only hoped so.

"She must have decided the diaries were safer hidden and lost forever than to fall into the wrong hands if they'd found her with them," Susannah had added as she'd passed the precious material into his hands.

"They're safe with me," he'd assured her, reacting to her uncertain look. "And you're safe now and out of this. You've done the right thing. We'll figure it out. We have to."

Gretchen, he thought, as he watched the tarmac rise to meet the jet. She'll need to see the rings. If anyone could decode the inscribed message, it would be her.

He dragged a hand through his hair, thought of the sister he hadn't known existed until Violet had told him mere weeks ago. Violet had named her Grace, but her name had been changed to Gretchen when she was adopted. Poor Gretchen had been so excited to learn of their biological mother. She was going to be crushed when he broke the news about Violet.

She'd left Jake over an hour ago and Susannah had done nothing but think about Travis ever since. Back at the Rocking H, she let herself into the house, leaned back against the door and prayed Jake was right. That she'd done the right thing. It was out of her hands now. She was out of the picture, felt confident in Jake Ingram's assurances that she was also out of harm's way.

"It's us they want," he'd told her as they'd baked under the July sun at the edge of the school grounds and discussed a woman who had meant so much to both of them. "With Violet dead, whatever threat she represented to the Coalition died with her."

Now it all caught up with her. For the first time since she found the diaries and decoded Vi's heart-breaking story, she broke down and grieved. For the life and love that eluded her, for Vi and all she'd endured, even for Vi's five children and the danger they faced because of their extraordinary powers.

She didn't stop to think about what she was doing. She simply didn't want to be alone right now. She picked up the phone and called the only person she truly trusted, even though she knew it was a trust he'd never return.

When he answered, all she could do was cry.

Travis flew into Susannah's driveway, worried out of his mind. She hadn't been hysterical when she'd called, but she'd been close. So close, she couldn't even tell him what was wrong. He was afraid, as he'd never been afraid before.

Something was horribly wrong. If that son of a bitch hurt her, he swore he'd track him down and neuter him with his bare hands. Ignoring the pain in his ankle, he hobbled up the steps and wrenched open her door.

His heart broke when he saw her. All of her strength, all he knew her to be, was depleted. Her head was down, and tears fell on the pale, slim hands she clutched in her lap as she sat on a kitchen chair.

He dropped to his knees in front of her. "What's wrong?"

When she didn't answer, he dragged her onto his lap and held her. He was afraid if he didn't, she'd fly apart. Or maybe he was afraid he would.

He'd never felt so helpless or useless or so protective. He'd tear the head off anyone who came within a mile of her right now.

He tipped her face to his, wiped away her tears with his thumbs and asked again, "Baby, what's wrong?"

"What...what if I lose the baby?" she asked miserably. "What if, like everyone else, this baby—" She broke off, stared beyond him, unable to say it.

"Nothing is going to happen to the baby. Nothing's going to happen to you. I'm not going to let it."

He didn't think about what came out of his mouth next. He didn't censor or consider or marshal the truth he'd known, but hadn't wanted to admit.

"I love you too much to let anything happen to you. I don't care. It doesn't matter if you still love that creep. That loser could never care about you like I do or he'd never have let you go in the first place.

"He can't take care of you like I can either and as soon as I get you to a doctor and get you checked out, I'm going to prove to you you'll never be sorry. If you'll just give me the chance to—"

She pressed her fingers to his lips, cutting him off. Tears spilled from her eyes. "You love me?"

He closed his eyes, swallowed. "God help me, I do."

"God help us both." She finally smiled and settled into his arms. She settled into home.

That night, wrapped up in each other, she told him the entire incredible story. She told him about the diaries, the rings, about Code Proteus and the Extraordinary Five and Vi's murder. Travis was incredulous, but he believed every word, especially about Jake Ingram.

It wasn't the baby's father she'd gone to see, after all.

"I should have known," he whispered against her hair, running his hand up and down along the bare length of her arm. "I should have known you better."

As she lay sleeping in his arms, he knew she was right. Until this situation was resolved, the truth of

Violet's death would have to remain a secret. And until then, he wasn't letting her out of his sight.

Sooner woke Trav around midnight. He heard her scratching at the bedroom door, whimpering softly.

Half asleep, he left Susannah tucked in bed and dreaming while he let the dog outside. Only she didn't want out. He turned on a light, then followed her to the living room. She led him to the closet where Boomer sat like a palace guard outside the slightly open door.

He knew before he looked inside what he'd find.

"Well, you finally decided to give 'em up, huh, girl?"

A squirming, fuzzy knot of grunting puppies wiggled and snuggled and rooted around on the blanket in the corner.

"What's going on?"

He turned as Susannah wandered, barefoot and sleepy, into the living room. He couldn't put a name to what he experienced when he saw her, sleep-mussed, softly female, the woman of his heart. He couldn't contain the aching warmth that spread through his chest and made it feel as if there wasn't enough room inside him to hold all the love.

He drew her against his side. Pressed a kiss to the top of her head as her arm wound around his waist. "We have guests."

"Oh. Oh," she cooed and after smiling into his face, dropped to her knees to hug Sooner and praise her for being a brave and wonderful mother.

"Six, I think," Trav said in answer to her unspoken question.

Together they watched as Sooner carefully circled

the precious puppies then lay down, curling her warmth around them.

"What a good momma," Susannah crooned.

It was too much suddenly. Too much love. Too much wonder. Too much to believe he could be so lucky to have found what he had in her. "Why is it different with me?" he asked abruptly.

She looked up, love shining on her face, her soft smile layered with confusion. "Why is *what* different with you?"

He held out a hand, drew her to her feet and against him. "Why do you know it's love with me?"

She leaned into the circle of his arms and framed his face with her hands. "Because you are everything they weren't," she whispered with a conviction as fierce as the love in her eyes. "Because you are everything I needed them to be."

And this woman, Trav knew, was everything he'd been afraid to believe in.

"I'll never leave you," he promised.

She rose up on her tiptoes and softly kissed him on the lips. "I know," she said with such simple and open honesty all he could do was smile.

Epilogue

The sky over Brunhia was a brooding, gunmetal gray. It matched Jake's mood as he looked into his sister Gretchen's eyes. They were the same blue as his. The same blue as Violet's, and today, they were misty with pain.

Gretchen looked from the gold-and-ruby rings clutched in her hand to her husband, Kurt, then back to Jake again.

"Who are these people? How could they do this? How could this happen? How could Vi have died before I ever got to meet her? To know her?"

It was difficult to watch a strong woman weep. Feeling helpless, Jake crammed his hands in his pockets and watched as Kurt moved to her side, wrapped her in his arms.

"The baby," Kurt said gently. "We'll name her Violet. And she'll be as beautiful and brave as both her mother and her grandmother."

"We have to find them," she whispered against his shoulder, clutching a handful of his shirt in her fingers. She looked up at Jake. "We have to stop them before they get to our missing siblings. Or us."

"We will," both men said as one, their gazes connecting over Gretchen's head and holding in sacred promise. "We will."

* * *

The technician grinned from Susannah to Travis as they watched the sonogram screen in the obstetrician's office. "Do you want to know the sex?"

The blue eyes that met Trav's were filled with excitement and hesitation. Already he knew her so well. She wanted to know, but she didn't want to spoil it for him if he wanted it to be a surprise.

"Yeah," he said and felt his lips curve up in response to her smile. "We want to know."

"You have a healthy little baby girl growing in there, Mom and Dad."

"A little girl." Susannah met his gaze, her joy overriding the technician's assumption that Travis was the father.

"Not *a* little girl," he said, placing a hand over her abdomen and the child sleeping there. "*Our* little girl."

The love shining in her eyes warmed him as he hadn't been warm in a very long time.

"Well, now you've done it. You're going to have me blubbering again."

He leaned over, kissed her gently. "Blubber away. I brought tissues."

Later, celebrating over lunch at a café in Steamboat Springs, they sat at a table by a window. The view of the mountains and the land they loved, where they planned to spend the rest of their lives together, was spectacular.

Susannah saw the covert and appreciative looks Travis received from the other women in the café. He was tall and tanned and so beautiful it made her chest hurt. He could have any woman he wanted, and here she was, growing as big as a barn, yet he only had eyes for her.

"Oh." Eyes widening with surprise, she met his startled gaze across the table. "Give me your hand. Quick."

His concerned scowl softened with wonder when she placed his hand over her abdomen. She knew the minute he felt it, too. The gentle swell of motion, a subtle rock and roll of their baby kicking.

She was strong, their child. *Their* child. She would grow happy and confident with their love to nurture her.

"Do you think Vi would mind if we named her Mae, after my mother?" she asked softly. "Actually, Mae Violet sounds beautiful together, doesn't it?"

He brought their joined hands to his lips, pressed a kiss to her knuckles and smiled. "It sounds beautiful. I think it would please Violet very much."

"And I think maybe it was fate—us finding each other," she said, looking lovingly into his eyes.

"Yeah," he agreed, his voice caressing her. "Fate has a way of looking out for dysfunctional souls."

"And for soul mates. We were meant to be together."

Sunlight glinted off the gold in his hair, gilding his lashes as he leaned close, touched his lips to hers, and told her without words that he couldn't agree with her more.

* * * * *

*There are more secrets to reveal—
don't miss out!*

*Coming in October 2003 to
Silhouette Books...*

*With her life in danger, Ambassador
Samantha Barnes thought that
Marcus Evans, the Navy SEAL suspected
of being one of the Extraordinary Five,
was her knight in shining armor,
until the lethal programming in his mind
was unlocked....*

HER BEAUTIFUL ASSASSIN
By Virginia Kantra

FAMILY SECRETS: *Five extraordinary
siblings. One dangerous past.
Unlimited potential.*

*And now,
for a sneak peek,
just turn the page...*

One

"We need to talk," Samantha Barnes, U.S. Ambassador to Delmonico said.

Lieutenant Marcus Evans sat beside her in the limo, his long-fingered hands lightly balancing his hat on his knees, looking good enough to be on a Navy recruiting poster or the stage at Chippendale's. Since her husband's death, she had closed herself off from everything but work, her feelings dulled, her senses deadened. But the lieutenant breached her safe, soft, stifling cocoon without even trying. The angles of his knees, the sheer size of his body, even the smell of him, hot male and uniform starch, encroached on her space.

"Yes, ma'am," he said politely.

She almost sighed. Did he have to be so gorgeous? And so young.

Practically young enough to be her— No, clearly not her son, she decided in relief, studying the power of his chest and arms, the maturity around his mouth. But young and fit and healthy enough to make her feel old and tired.

"What you said today to Senator Twitchell…" She hesitated.

"He was the blowhard, right?"

She bit the inside of her cheek to keep from agreeing with him. "It was inappropriate. In future, I would prefer that you not express your opinions about the deployment of U.S. troops in Europe. You have no understanding of the intricacies involved.''

He stiffened on the broad bench seat, but his tone was perfectly even. ''With respect, ma'am, I may not know much about your job, but I do understand military service.''

Of course he did.

''I'm not questioning your grasp of the military realities,'' Samantha said softly. ''Only your grasp of the political ones.''

He regarded her for a moment, his blue eyes bright in his tanned face. ''Fair enough.'' He smiled. The impact knocked the air from her lungs. ''Anything else?''

Samantha inhaled carefully. ''There is one more thing. When we were saying farewell, why did you get between me and Senator Dobson?''

Marcus shrugged. ''He was too close. I didn't like the way he was crowding you.''

Embarrassment washed her cheeks and flooded her stomach. She hadn't liked it, either. John Dobson had definitely taken advantage of the pretend intimacy of a political embrace to let his hands wander. But she hadn't thought anyone else had noticed. Much better, in her experience, for her not to notice, too.

''It was a little awkward,'' she admitted. ''But it's less awkward if we simply ignore it. You need to be something of an invisible partner at these events, I'm afraid.''

The lieutenant shook his head. ''No.''

She felt her jaw drop. ''Excuse me?''

''You want me to keep my mouth shut, fine,'' he said. ''But I'm supposed to be your bodyguard. And as long as I'm guarding your body, I'm not going to let some guy play grab ass with you.''

He took her breath away. His blunt defense was completely unexpected.

Totally unacceptable.

Utterly disarming.

She firmed her lips. ''I'm a diplomat, Lieutenant. I cover my own ass. Your job is to protect me from more serious threats.''

He didn't even bother to answer her.

SILHOUETTE Romance

Escape to a place where a kiss is still a kiss...

Feel the breathless connection...

Fall in love as though it were

the very first time...

Experience the power of love!

Come to where favorite authors—such as

Diana Palmer, Stella Bagwell,

Marie Ferrarella and many more—

deliver heart-warming romance and genuine

emotion, time after time after time....

Silhouette Romance—

stories straight from the heart!

Silhouette®

Where love comes alive™

Where love comes alive™

SILHOUETTE *Romance*™

From first love to forever, these love stories are
for today's woman with traditional values.

Silhouette® **Desire**

A highly passionate, emotionally powerful
and always provocative read.

SPECIAL EDITION™

Emotional, compelling stories that capture the
intensity of living, loving and creating a family in
today's world.

Silhouette®

INTIMATE MOMENTS™

A roller-coaster read that delivers romantic thrills
in a world of suspense, adventure and more.